The offer was so tempting.

In that instant, she would have given anything to be able to trust him. All of a sudden, more than ever before, she realized just how tired she was. Tired of running, tired of looking over her shoulder everywhere she went. It was an infinite road with no end in sight.

She would give anything to be able to trust someone, anyone, for the first time in so long, to turn her face into that broad chest, to ease her burden onto one of those shoulders and let someone else carry the load, if only for a short time.

She didn't say a word. There was nothing she could say, nothing Ross would understand, that wouldn't require explanations she couldn't give. Instead, she turned away and escaped into the bathroom, the moment over. Reality had set in, offering the cold reminder that she couldn't trust this man, or any other.

KERRY CONNOR

STRANGERS IN THE NIGHT

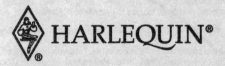

HARLEQUIN®

TORONTO • NEW YORK • LONDON
AMSTERDAM • PARIS • SYDNEY • HAMBURG
STOCKHOLM • ATHENS • TOKYO • MILAN • MADRID
PRAGUE • WARSAW • BUDAPEST • AUCKLAND

This book is dedicated with gratitude to everyone who
ever told me they enjoyed something I wrote (even when
I suspected they were just being kind) for that little bit of
encouragement I needed to keep going.
Your words meant the world to me and helped me find
my own. Thank you.

ISBN-13: 978-0-373-69334-4
ISBN-10:   0-373-69334-6

STRANGERS IN THE NIGHT

Copyright © 2008 by Kerry Connor

www.eHarlequin.com

Printed in U.S.A.

ABOUT THE AUTHOR

A lifelong mystery reader, Kerry Connor first discovered romantic suspense by reading Harlequin Intrigue books and is thrilled to be writing for the line. Kerry lives and writes in Southern California.

Books by Kerry Connor

HARLEQUIN INTRIGUE
1067—STRANGERS IN THE NIGHT

CAST OF CHARACTERS

Allie Freeman—A witness to murder.

Gideon Ross—The bounty hunter was tracking a criminal when he found a woman running for her life.

Kathleen Mulroney—Her murder set everything in motion.

Price Chastain—The real estate mogul had gotten away with plenty of crimes—and intended to get away with this one.

Roy Taylor—Ross's nemesis was hunting prey of his own.

Ken Newcomb—Ross's NYPD contact.

Dominick Brancato—A man with a mission of his own.

Prologue

The taxi rolled to a stop next to the Chastain building just after nine o'clock.

For a moment Allie sat there, listening to the raindrops patter against the roof of the cab, staring out through the liquid-smeared window into the darkness. She knew there was a light burning directly above the door she planned to use to enter the building. The veil of rain obscured it, making the alley between the Manhattan high-rise and its neighbor appear utterly black.

Naturally she'd forgotten to bring an umbrella. It had been that kind of day.

The driver twisted in his seat and shot her a skeptical glance. "You sure you don't want me to take you around the front?"

The only thing Allie was sure about was that this was the last place she wanted to be. She was exhausted. Her back was killing her; her feet ached. All she wanted was to sink back against the cushioned seat and have him take her home.

But she'd made the mistake of doing her brother a favor and getting him tickets for tomorrow's Mets game, then compounded the error by leaving them on her desk. That was what she got for being in such a hurry to leave work on a Friday in the first place. Of course, with her luck it had to be an early-afternoon game. For her brother and his buddies to get to the ballpark in time, she either had to come back to work tonight or make the trip early in the morning. After the week she'd had, there was no way she was getting out of bed before noon tomorrow.

She reached into her purse for the fare. "This is fine."

"You want me to wait?"

"No." She'd be lucky to afford the fare back to Queens without paying him to sit there while she ran inside. She'd have to try to hail another taxi when she got out.

Shoving the money into the driver's open palm and ignoring the look that said he clearly thought she had a few screws loose, Allie stepped out of the cab. A few seconds later it pulled away.

She moved quickly down the alley, muttering under her breath about baseball and younger brothers. She only hoped that by using the back service entrance and bypassing security in the front, she could get in and out faster. One of the night guards who often manned the front desk was a creep. She had no idea if he was working tonight, but wasn't about to risk it.

The rain continued to fall, and she was nearly soaked by the time she spotted the dim light above the back entrance up ahead. A sigh of relief whooshed from between her teeth. More than ready to get inside, she reached into her pocket for the security code she wasn't supposed to have. It was good to have friends in high places, in this case Nadine in Payroll. Nadine wasn't supposed to have it, either, but Allie wasn't about to rat her out.

Her hand had just closed around the slip of paper when she heard voices.

The sound was so unexpected she missed a step and nearly stumbled. She reached out and steadied herself against the wall, and hesitated, uncertain. She couldn't make out who was speaking, but they were definitely coming from in front of her—right where she was headed.

Curious in spite of herself, Allie slowly moved closer. She could make the voices out now, hushed and angry. She realized with a start that one belonged to Price Chastain himself. Real-estate mogul. Head of the Chastain Corporation. The man whose name was on her paycheck, even though she was more likely to see him in the newspaper than in the office. Surprise drew her up short again. He was just about the last person she'd expect to be hanging out in an alley. The other voice belonged to a woman. Allie didn't recognize it. Whoever she was, though, she was holding up her end of the argument. Chastain's temper was legendary, but the woman was giving it right back.

Moving on tiptoe, Allie peered around the corner to the recessed back entrance.

They were standing directly in front of the door she'd intended to use, clearly illuminated in a puddle of light. Mr. Chastain was right in the woman's face. She stood in profile, allowing Allie to identify her. Her name was Kathleen… something. Allie wasn't sure what department she worked in. She only knew her well enough to recognize her face. The woman was shaking, her hands fisted at her sides, her face dark with rage. She didn't back down from whatever Chastain was saying.

They weren't alone, either. Two other men stood slightly behind the woman on either side. Something about their stance said that despite their location, they weren't there to back her up.

An uneasy feeling slid down Allie's spine. She didn't know what was going on and she didn't want to. The last thing she needed was to get mixed up in something that was none of her business. She'd have to suck it up and go in the front entrance. At the moment all she wanted was to get out of there. That sole purpose fueling her movements, she began to inch backward in the direction she'd come from.

Just as Mr. Chastain pulled out a gun.

For a split second, time stood still. Allie froze. Kathleen froze. The air that had been charged with angry voices was now stunningly quiet.

Then Allie noticed that time, somehow, was still moving. Mr. Chastain was still moving. He'd produced a gun from his coat with a casualness that seemed wildly out of place for the situation, the same ease with which he raised the gun, aimed it directly at the chest of the woman standing in front of him.

And fired.

Like a video running in slow motion suddenly propelled into fast forward, everything seemed to happen at once. The muffled shot. The eruption of blood that splattered across Mr. Chastain's pristine silk suit and overcoat. Kathleen's head snapping back, eyes wide with shock, before she fell to the ground.

And then, once more, silence. Nothing but the steady beat of the rain.

A scream rose in Allie's throat, pressing at her Adam's apple with a force that begged to be released. Some deep-seated sense of self-preservation prevented it. She clamped her lips together in a tight line to keep the sound from escaping. She couldn't scream, couldn't afford to let him know she'd seen.

So she stood there, hidden in the alley's shadows, afraid to move, afraid not to. She watched as Mr. Chastain slowly lowered the gun and returned it to his pocket.

Murder. I just witnessed a murder.

Allie stared at his expression, no less horrified by what she saw there than by what she'd seen him do. There was no remorse. There was no anger. There was…nothing. If she hadn't seen him kill someone, she never would have believed it. He gazed down at the woman's body with an expression so blank that she almost wondered if he realized what he'd done.

Then, with a chilling coolness, he smiled.

He said something to the two men, who'd stood there the whole time and done nothing. One of them laughed.

Fresh horror swept over her. Allie slowly became aware of the fact that she was shaking. Tremors racked her body from head to foot. Silent tears mingled with the rain and poured down her cheeks, blurring her vision, the result of keeping that scream inside. She couldn't wipe them away, couldn't move at all. Then she realized to her horror that she was still standing there.

How long had it been? Ten seconds? Minutes? An hour? Too long.

She had to go. He might glance over and see her at any moment.

And then he would kill her, too.

Oh, God.

She had to go. She had to run.

Holding her breath, doing her best not to make a sudden movement, she inched backward, retreating farther into the shadows. She ducked around the corner. Then, only then, did she start moving faster, spinning on her heel, hurtling into the darkness and the escape that lay beyond.

And she ran, so hard and so fast it seemed as though she would never stop running again.

Chapter One

One Year Later

Gideon Ross heard the vehicle a good couple of minutes before it emerged from the winding mountain road and rolled to a stop out front. There was never any doubt where it was headed. His cabin was the only destination on this particular road. Most days passed without a single engine marring the silence, the town store's monthly deliveries being the only exception. After a couple weeks of trying to be neighborly, the few residents of the town at the base of the mountain who'd even bothered had taken the hint and given up. The cabin was too remote and its owner even more so to make the effort worthwhile.

It was a lesson they'd learned none too soon for his tastes. Ross hadn't bought the isolated cabin deep in the Adirondacks in hopes of meeting people. He'd moved here to get away from them. If he could find a way to bypass those supply deliveries that didn't involve starvation, he'd gladly take it.

He knew long before it arrived that the vehicle making its way up the mountain wasn't the store's delivery truck. He was well acquainted with the sound of its engine. This ominous and steadily rising growl wasn't it.

Lifting the beer bottle to his mouth, he finished off the last few ounces, then dropped it to the floor beside him. With his feet propped up on the porch railing and the chair tipped back on two legs, he folded his hands behind his head. To hell with it. He wasn't about to let some idiot ruin his day. The autumn afternoon was too warm and the sun felt too good to get worked up about much of anything.

The vehicle—late-model Buick, he registered before he even thought about it—stopped a few feet in front of the cabin. The engine was cut off, and a few seconds later he heard someone climb out.

He didn't bother to remove the fishing hat he'd tugged low over his face to see who it was. He knew two things without looking. Whoever it was didn't know him, because they would know better than to bother him, and they weren't welcome. They'd figure that one out for themselves soon enough.

Footsteps crunched along the rocks and gravel until they hit the front steps. It was a man, or a woman who walked like one. From the sound of it, a man who was carrying more than a little excess weight.

Ross would have groaned if it hadn't meant giving away that he wasn't sleeping. Old habits died hard, and a year of rust hadn't kept him from analyzing every detail without intending to. As long as the visitor didn't intend him harm, it didn't matter who it was. He was an easy target and he wasn't dead yet. Things looked fairly promising on that front.

"You going to stop faking and offer an old man a drink?"

So much for promising. The voice was familiar, but no more welcome than when the visitor had been a stranger. Tension coiled in the pit of his stomach, killing the beer buzz he'd been working on all afternoon.

"Well?" the voice demanded.

"No."

The porch railing creaked, no doubt from the strain of Ken Newcomb leaning against it. "Too bad. I haven't been driving for six hours for nothing."

"Plenty of places back in the city to get a beer."

"Except you're out here in the middle of the damn wilderness."

"There's a reason for that."

"Yeah. Because you've lost your damn mind."

"Because I want to be left alone."

"I would be happy not to be here. I wouldn't be, either, if you had a phone."

"There's nobody I'm interested in talking to."

"Well, you're going to want to talk to me. I've got a job for you."

"Not interested."

"You will be."

"I let my license lapse. You're going to have to find yourself another bounty hunter."

"You don't need a license. This isn't official. It's personal."

That was what Ross was afraid of.

He finally pushed back the brim of his hat and peered up at his visitor. The homicide detective had a face the texture of tanned leather, seeming to bear the evidence of every case he'd ever worked in twenty-five years on the job. In the scant fourteen months since Ross had last seen him, Newcomb appeared to have acquired a good five years more on that face. Fresh lines were carved into his forehead and around his eyes. His gaze simmered with fevered emotion.

The knot in the pit of Ross's stomach tightened. Whatever it was the man wanted, it was big. That was going to make it even harder to say no to him.

Which didn't mean Ross wouldn't do it.

When he didn't say anything, Newcomb continued, "Did you hear about Chastain?"

Price Chastain. The name was enough to kill the last of the peace Newcomb's arrival hadn't managed to dispel. "I heard."

"Trial starts in a couple of weeks. I thought I might see you back in the city for it."

"Newcomb, how many times has the D.A. indicted Chastain for something?"

Newcomb's hesitation was telling. "Four."

"And how many convictions has he gotten?"

"None."

"So you can understand why I didn't hightail it back to the city this time."

"It's different this time. We've got him."

"I've heard that before."

"This time we've got him on tape."

Ross let that sink in, more the excitement in Newcomb's voice than the words themselves. He wasn't going to get his hopes up, but it wasn't like Newcomb was going anywhere. "I'm listening."

"How much have you heard about the case?"

"We don't get much news from the city up in these parts," he drawled.

"Victim's Kathleen Mulroney, a secretary at his company. On a Friday night last September he caught her trying to sneak out of the building with some files she'd copied. We don't know what was in them. They were long gone by the time the arrest was made. Computer records show she copied some kind of hidden files, but Chastain had already moved them by the time we got there. We think she stumbled on evidence of his dirty dealings."

"You don't have a concrete motive."

"Doesn't matter. That'll be good enough."

Ross decided to withhold judgment on that. "Go on."

"He must have been on to her, because he was waiting for

her when she came out of the building. He confronted her, they argued, and he shot her in the chest."

"The bastard did her himself?" This was too good to be true. Exactly why Ross wasn't buying it yet.

"Yep. Probably in a fit of rage, possibly out of sheer arrogance. We've never been able to pin anything else on him. What's one more murder?"

"And you got this on tape?"

"What Chastain didn't know was the building across the alley had just had a new security system installed. A camera above its back entrance captured the whole thing. If it hadn't, she would have just been somebody else connected to Chastain who disappeared without a trace. We'd have never been able to connect him to it." Newcomb shook his head. "Five years of investigating the bastard, and we get him out of dumb luck."

"Isn't that always the way?" Ross muttered.

As if sensing Ross's lack of enthusiasm, Newcomb elaborated. "We've got everything. Chastain catching the Mulroney woman coming out of the building. The argument. Chastain shooting her. Two of his men removing the body."

"Which men?"

"A guy you never heard of, new on Chastain's payroll, Pete Crowley." Newcomb met his gaze head-on. "And Roy Taylor."

A cold trickle slid down Ross's spine. "Why are you here, Newcomb?"

"Taylor skipped town."

Newcomb didn't have to say another word. They both knew it. Those three words told Ross everything he needed to know—and guaranteed his cooperation. He swore, exactly the reaction the detective was looking for. For the first time since he'd arrived, Newcomb smiled, a deep satisfied grin.

Ross closed his eyes before he put his fist right in the middle of those grinning teeth.

RESTLESS, ROSS PULLED a fresh beer out of the fridge and popped the cap off with the back of his thumb. There wasn't a chance of getting his buzz back, but if anything called for a drink, this was it. He just wished he had something stronger on hand.

Draining half the bottle in one pull, he paced a ragged path across the cabin's hardwood floors while he waited for Newcomb to emerge from the bathroom. The man was taking so long in there he must have been guzzling coffee for the entire drive here.

Part of him wanted to throw the detective all the way back to the city and forget everything he'd been told. Getting pulled back into this mess was the last thing he needed. He'd finally made his escape, bought the spread in the back of beyond he'd been dreaming about for years and made a clean break with his former profession. For the past year, he'd managed to find, if not peace, then at least quiet. No more tracking skips into places no sane person would go, no more dealing with the lowlifes and the overworked, understaffed law enforcement that populated New York. Here he was left alone, and that was all he really wanted.

All except to see Price Chastain behind bars.

Ross lifted the bottle to his mouth again. The alcohol burned as it went down. The sensation was nothing compared to the anger that burned in his gut at the thought of Chastain finally getting what he deserved.

Price Malcolm Chastain, born Gary Allan Paine, a self-made real-estate magnate who owned a sizable chunk of three boroughs. A glorified slumlord who'd expanded his empire by whatever dirty means necessary. Not to mention an all-around sleazebag, a man with almost as many under-world connections as the mob.

And the person who'd ordered the death of Jed Walsh, the man who'd taught Ross everything he knew and the only person in the world who'd given a damn about him when Ross was nothing but a kid scrambling to get by on the streets.

Of course neither Chastain nor Taylor, his head enforcer, had been charged for anything related to Jed's death. There'd been no way to prove what everyone knew had happened. That was how it was with Chastain. More than one person who'd stood in the man's way had wound up dead over the years, yet trouble slid off him like rainwater off a slanted roof. The feds were after him. The New York attorney general wanted a piece of him. After being made a fool of four times, the D.A. would kill for a conviction.

Yet nothing stuck. Ross wasn't green enough to think the bad guys always got what was coming to them. As much as it stung, he'd finally had to face the fact that Chastain's reckoning wasn't coming anytime soon.

Maybe he should have held on to some of that old optimism this time.

The bathroom door swung open. Newcomb stepped out into the main room, tightening his belt with both hands. He cast an appreciative eye around the space.

"I wouldn't have thought it, but this is a nice setup you've got for yourself here. Got myself a bit of land out in Jersey I'm going to develop if I ever get around to retiring. Maybe that day'll be coming sooner rather than later, huh?"

That same hard gleam, the glitter of satisfaction, burned in Newcomb's eyes. That Newcomb was so sure Chastain was going down only stoked Ross's impatience.

If anyone but Ken Newcomb had shown up on his doorstep, Ross wouldn't have given him the time of day. He wasn't that comfortable around cops to begin with, despite all the years they'd spent ostensibly working on the same side of the law. He'd spent too many years in his youth outrunning them to feel at ease around them. It was part of what made him so good at his job; he knew what someone desper-ate to elude the law would do and where he would go. But Newcomb had been the lead detective on Jed's case, as well as a member of that elite group that wanted Chastain to go down as badly as Ross did, if not more.

"When?" Ross said, cutting right to it.

"Two days, we think." He eyed the now-empty bottle Ross cradled in both hands. "You got another one of those?"

Ross stalked over to the refrigerator without missing a beat. "You *think?*"

Newcomb's face darkened. "Taylor was supposed to be in court yesterday morning. His lawyer tried covering for him, but it took us about two seconds to figure out he wasn't in the city anymore."

"I'd say that was a couple hours too late. You should've had a man on him. You had to know he was going to run. He shouldn't have even been out on bail."

"You know it and I know it. Try telling that to the judge."

Ross plunked an unopened bottle of beer on the table in front of Newcomb. "Who is it?"

The detective shook his head as he reached for the bottle, and Ross knew he'd understood the question he'd really been asking. Chastain had gotten away with too much for too long not to have greased a few palms along the way.

"Bernstein's on the up-and-up," Newcomb said. "Real hard-nosed law-and-order type. The D.A. was glad to get him. Besides, we were more concerned about Chastain running. He has a lot more to lose."

"The case is that strong?" After the way Chastain had weaseled out of every charge ever brought against him, Ross couldn't imagine him consigning himself to a life on the lam unless he was sure he was going down. And Chastain wasn't one to concede easily.

Newcomb ticked off the evidence on his fingers. "We've

got the blood on his suit and overcoat. And we've got the tape."

"It's that good, huh?"

Newcomb took a drink before answering. For the first time Ross sensed a crack in the detective's confidence. "What?"

Newcomb heaved a sigh. "We don't have a body, though witnesses spotted Taylor dumping something in the river that night. There's no sound on the tape of course, which would help lock down the motive if we could hear what they were saying. Plus, it was kind of rainy that night, so Chastain's lawyer's probably going to argue we can't see everything clear to enough to be absolutely sure. Reasonable doubt—you know the drill. His lawyer's going to try everything he can."

"So much for that slam dunk, huh?"

Newcomb glowered at him through bloodshot eyes. "He pulls out a gun, shoots her in the chest, she goes down, they drag the body away. It's all there in black and white. Short of an eyewitness, it's the best case we're going to get."

"Why would Taylor run and not Chastain?"

Newcomb swallowed deeply from the bottle and pulled it away from his lips with a satisfied sigh. "Maybe Chastain still thinks he's getting off scot-free. He's a cocky SOB. Taylor's just a hired gun. He has to know it doesn't look good. He can either turn on Chastain or he can run. And the last guy who tried to rat out Chastain on this turned up dead."

"Who?"

"Crowley, the other guy who'd removed Mulroney's body with Taylor that night. He'd made some noises about wanting to talk to the D.A. Then he turned up dead. Everybody knows who did it."

"But no way to prove it."

Newcomb tipped his bottle in acknowledgment.

"So Crowley's death left Taylor alone to stand trial with Chastain."

"And maybe Taylor finally figured out that his chances of walking away this time weren't looking so good."

"Who's on the case? Officially, that is."

"Wes Miller."

Ross nodded. He knew the other skip tracer. "He's good. He shouldn't have trouble finding Taylor. You don't need me."

"Miller's good. You're the best."

"Jed was the best."

"And he taught you everything he knew. More important, you've got more incentive than Miller. He's only in this for the money. This is personal for you. You want Taylor to go down even more than you want Chastain to, and you won't stop until he's back here where he belongs. We both know it. That's why I'm here."

Damn. Newcomb knew him too well. He knew that while Chastain was the man in charge, Taylor was the one Ross held responsible for Jed's death.

His control over his emotions must have slipped. When he looked up from the table, he found Newcomb staring at him, that strange triumphant glow in his eyes. "So you'll do it?"

Say no.

The words came automatically.

"I'll do it."

Ross didn't know who he'd been trying to convince otherwise. Deep down, though part of him never would admit it, he wanted to do this. He hadn't been able to do anything for Jed when it mattered, hadn't been able to save his life, hadn't been able to see to it that the man responsible paid. But he could do this. This was what he was good at, what Jed had taught him to do. It only seemed right that his specialty be put to use to capture the man who'd killed Jed.

If he was completely honest with himself, he might admit he was looking forward to getting back into the game. Peace could be damned boring.

"You know, Newcomb, you didn't say anything about bringing him back in one piece."

Newcomb grinned slowly. "As long as there's enough of him to stand trial, he's all yours."

Chapter Two

"Good night, Connie," Mr. Mortimer said, holding the door of the pharmacy open to let her pass. "See you tomorrow."

"Good night," the woman he knew as Connie Baker echoed softly. She stepped past him onto the rain-slicked street, but try as she might, she couldn't force herself to repeat the latter sentiment.

She wouldn't be in to work tomorrow or ever again. By morning, she would be far from Chicago, leaving no trace of her short time here and Mr. Mortimer to wonder what had happened to his young cashier. Connie Baker would cease to exist, just another name to be discarded and never used again, like all the others. Beth Roberts. Lisa Greene. Allie Freeman. Just another woman who disappeared, never to be seen again, while another woman appeared out of nowhere in another place.

She didn't know why it was so hard to tell one more lie to a man she'd been dishonest with from the beginning. He didn't know her real name; he didn't know her past. He knew nothing about her but the carefully crafted story she'd chosen to tell him, and not one bit of it the truth.

Still, there was something about having her final words to him be yet another lie, even if she was the only one who would know. He'd been exceptionally good to her when she'd thought herself hardened against even the slightest human kindness. Louis Mortimer had owned his pharmacy in this neighborhood on the South Side of Chicago for forty years while raising three children here with his late wife, Marie. He'd given her a chance and asked few questions, sensing she was running from something.

It didn't seem right to leave without saying something. Nothing to tip him off now of course, but something he could consider later and know she hadn't meant to deceive him.

She started to turn back. "Mr. Mortimer—"

A rumble of thunder, either a remnant of the storm that had passed through that afternoon or a harbinger of a new one moving in, drowned out her words. By the time it passed, he'd already closed the door. One by one the interior lights flickered off, leaving her alone outside in the dark.

A wave of sadness crashed over her. She didn't know why. He wasn't the first person she hadn't had a chance to say a proper goodbye to. She knew better than to think he would be the last.

The thunder came again, far too quickly after the last rumble for comfort's sake. She lifted her face up to the sky in time to see a jagged bolt of lightning streak across the velvet darkness. There was no mistaking it. Another storm was moving in. Another reason for her to hurry, and she already had enough of those. Pushing her melancholy thoughts to the back of her mind, she began to walk.

Fog rolled across the street, obscuring the other businesses closed for the night. Perfect weather for Halloween, she thought, with the holiday two weeks away. It was less than perfect for her already frayed nerves.

She moved quickly, chased by a cold wind that bit into her too-thin coat and chilled her to the bone. She didn't worry about bumping into anyone. There were few people on the street at eleven o'clock on a Tuesday night. Other than the bar halfway down the block, none of the businesses on the strip were open this late.

Mr. Mortimer had often worried about her walking alone at night and had offered to walk her home. She'd done her best to convince him she'd be fine. She wasn't worried about being out by herself. With the sheer number of people who were looking for her, the idea that she would fall victim to a simple mugging defied belief.

Tonight, though, she couldn't help the feeling of unease that clawed up her spine and had her peering through the murky grayness and searching the shadows more thoroughly than usual for any sign of harm. She was more aware of the danger than ever before. It seemed to surround her, closing in like the fog with each passing moment.

She'd been following Chastain's trial, reading the New York papers at the nearest branch of the Chicago Public Library every couple of days. Just that morning she'd learned that Roy Taylor had skipped town two weeks before the trial was set to begin, and she knew why.

He was coming after her. She doubted he would have taken such a drastic step if he hadn't picked up her trail. And that meant she had to get out of Chicago ASAP.

She passed the bar, too lost in her thoughts to notice the noise and the lights coming from inside. She should have left as soon as she read the story, which had already been a few days old. She knew that now. At the time the risk of staying one more day had seemed worth it. She needed her last week's pay. The amount she had tucked away in her apartment would get her out of town, but not far enough that he wouldn't be able to find her again—and soon. So she'd made the decision to linger just one more night.

She just had to hope it wasn't a decision she ended up paying for.

She didn't know exactly what warned her. It could have

been a shadow shifting where there should have been nothing, or the soft scrape of shoes against pavement on what should have been a deserted street. All that mattered was that she suddenly knew she wasn't alone.

Someone was following her.

Her heart lurched in her chest. She forced herself to keep her steps even, as steady as they'd been before that moment of intuition. There was no way to tell how far away he was or where exactly he was lurking. Still, she struggled to listen over the pounding of her heart. Even the slightest sound offered a vital clue to her pursuer's location.

He was behind her.

How far?

Five feet?

Ten?

It was impossible to tell. He could be on her back in an instant.

The only advantage she had was that he didn't know she was aware of his presence. He planned to catch her off guard. Her only chance was to do the same to him first.

Her mind raced through every option. Then she remembered. There was an alley up ahead, maybe only fifteen steps away. She couldn't see it now, hidden in the gloom. But she knew it was there. He didn't. That would make all the difference.

In her head she ticked off the steps, hoping her count was close. One. Then five. Ten. Only a measure of control she hadn't known she possessed kept her from running.

She counted the last remaining steps, her breath hitching in her throat. One. Two. Three. Four.

And there it was.

Go!

She cut around the corner and broke into an all-out run.

Almost immediately, she heard the muffled curse, a confused noise, then the sound of someone bursting into the alley behind her.

She didn't look back or slow for an instant. The alley was dark, dank and cramped, ripe with the odors of garbage and the sewer. She noticed none of it, couldn't hear him behind her, couldn't hear anything but the pounding of her shoes on the pavement. The close walls echoed the sound. He wouldn't be able to tell how near she was or how far.

And there was no way for her to tell where the end of the alley was. The street it intersected was primarily residential, with almost no lights illuminating the road. So she kept running through the darkness, toward the darkness. She didn't know until she suddenly cleared the smells and felt the open air wash over her that she was free.

And still she didn't stop. Her apartment building was to the left. She cut right, back toward the well-lit business district she'd left behind. He wouldn't be expecting her to do that. He'd expect her to head in the direction she'd originally been going. He needed her to. It would be easier for him to take her where there were fewer people, little chance that someone would interfere. That was why he hadn't taken her on the street, had tried to follow her home. That was exactly why she couldn't.

She took another right into the next alley, then another, working her way blindly through a network of back streets that should lead her back to the one where she'd begun. There would be people at the bar. If she could just get back there, she would be safe. He wouldn't dare come after her in there. He didn't want to involve the police any more than she did. She just had to get to the bar.

And when she finally spotted the phosphorescent glow that signaled the main street was up ahead, she picked up one last burst of speed, running straight for its blessed safety. She reached it within seconds, her heart thudding, nothing but hope and adrenaline coursing through her veins. Breaking through, she darted around the corner.

And straight into a wall.

A blast of cold water couldn't have been more of a shock. She bounced back, stumbling unevenly, off balance. Hands reached out to grip her forearms.

Startled, scared, she lifted her head and found herself staring into a face that was partially hidden in shadow.

Not a wall.

A man.

Fog billowed around him, rendering him nothing but a menacing silhouette that loomed over her. It didn't matter. She knew from the unyielding hold he had on her arms that he wasn't about to let her go.

She should have known Taylor wouldn't be alone.

He was one of them. He had to be.

Her limbs froze just when she needed them to fight back the most. After running for so long, it seemed impossible to believe the moment of reckoning had arrived.

They'd caught her.

"YOU JUST MISSED him. Left not ten minutes ago."

Ross barely heard the bartender over the raucous noise filling the bar, but he got the message loud and clear. He bit back a curse. He couldn't afford to indulge the instinct, couldn't risk offending the bartender when the man held information he needed. It wasn't the man's fault that he didn't have the answer Ross wanted to hear. That didn't make it any easier to take.

He had to wait to question the man further. The bartender turned away to refill the glass of a man at the other end of the bar. The small neighborhood pub was surprisingly crowded for a Tuesday night. The bartender and a single waitress were the only ones working. Ross was lucky to get the man's attention at all, especially since he wasn't drinking.

Impatience gnawed at him all the same. It rankled that he'd managed to track Taylor down to this bar, only to miss him by ten minutes.

It had been far easier to find Taylor than he'd expected, so much so the situation made Ross a little uneasy. For someone on the run, Taylor hadn't done a very good job covering his tracks as he'd cut an uneven path from New York to Chicago. Despite the head start the man had on him, it had only taken Ross a few days to catch up.

The bartender finally swung back in his direction. Ross motioned him over. "How long was this guy in here?" he asked, tapping the photo of Taylor he'd placed on the bar.

The bartender heaved a sigh that sent his belly quaking and considered the question. "Three hours or so. Sat at the table by the window there. Had four beers."

"Was he alone?"

"Yep. Just sat there. Didn't talk much. Kept his eyes on that window."

"He leave alone?"

"I didn't see him leave. One minute he was there, and the next, when I turned around, he was gone."

The bartender was eyeing his patrons down the length of the bar, and Ross knew he was about to lose him. Figuring he'd gotten all he was going to out of the man, he pulled a bill out of his wallet and placed it on the counter. The bartender accepted it without a word. Ross moved away from the bar and headed for the door.

Outside, he glanced in both directions down the street, trying to gauge which way Taylor might have gone. There was no one in sight. To the left were a couple of businesses, their windows shuttered, the lights dimmed. There was a laundromat, a drugstore. Nothing he could imagine Taylor being interested in.

To the right lay houses and apartment buildings, what was mainly a residential area. The windows were mostly dark, their inhabitants safe in their beds for the night.

The bartender's comment that Taylor had stared through a window for hours bothered him. Instead of choosing a more discreet position in the back of the bar where it was unlikely anyone would see him, he'd chosen a seat right in front of the window. Either he really wasn't worried about being spotted—and Ross knew Taylor was too savvy to be so careless—or he was looking for someone. Undoubtedly the same someone he'd come all this way to find.

At this time of night Ross was inclined to believe someone would be heading home, instead of to any of the closed businesses to his left. He headed right.

Thunder rumbled overhead. Ross flipped up the collar on his leather jacket, but didn't try to seek cover. He moved quickly. There was the possibility that Taylor had driven off, having completed whatever business had brought him here. Ross refused to consider that yet. He wouldn't accept that he'd been this close only to lose the man again. He had to be somewhere nearby.

Distracted by his thoughts, Ross heard the running footsteps a heartbeat too late. He took an instinctive step back, but not quickly enough to avoid the person who barreled straight into him from out of nowhere.

Too slow, man.

His hands automatically went up to steady the person. One touch, and he knew it was a woman.

Then she threw her head up, a curtain of ebony hair flying back from her face. The lights were behind him, cutting through the gloom, offering him a clear view of her expression.

Huge, frightened eyes blinked up at him. Sure she was about to bolt, he tightened his hold on her arms.

He quickly took stock of the situation, spotting the alley she'd come out of, the opening so tucked away in the shadows he never would have noticed it.

He could feel her pulse beneath his thumbs, the double-time throb of her heart beneath the thin layers of her clothing. Combined with the look of shock in her eyes, it was obvious she was terrified. Of him?

When she said nothing, he shook her gently. "Lady, are you all right?"

It took a second. Some of the fear in her eyes faded, replaced by confusion. She blinked and shook her head as though trying to clear it. He wondered if she was on drugs, only to dismiss the idea a moment later. Her eyes were clear and unerringly focused on his face. Her gaze was probing, searching his features for something, some semblance of familiarity, he supposed. She wouldn't find any. He never forgot a face, and he knew they'd never met.

"You're not one of them," she murmured, the words little more than a whisper carried on the wind. Still, there was something about her voice…

"One of who?" He regretted asking as soon as the words were out. Whatever this woman was into, he wasn't interested. He had problems enough of his own without worrying about someone else's. He needed to extricate himself from her situation, not dig in deeper. With each passing second, Taylor was getting that much farther away.

Before she could answer, the sounds of footsteps pounding down the alley she'd just emerged from reached them. No doubt whoever she was running from coming after her.

They both glanced toward the sound. She whipped her head back to face him a split second later. Steely determination had replaced the fear in her eyes, the transformation so complete she seemed to have become an entirely different person. He stared stupidly at the new stranger she'd become.

"Help me," she said, her voice as forceful as her expression. "Don't let him find me."

She'd managed to surprise him for the second time in half as many seconds. Not because of her demand or the sudden strength of her voice. No, it was her accent, now unmistakable and wholly out of place in this Midwestern city.

She was from New York.

She didn't give him a chance to process that simple fact. With one more glance over her shoulder, she threw her arms around his neck and pulled him flat against her. At the same time, she twisted, throwing them both back into a small recess in the wall, so that he was pinning her against it.

He understood immediately. Anyone who came out of that alley would likely pass by without even knowing they were there.

And if he did…

Her hands wound themselves into his hair, pulling his head close. For a moment, he was sure she was going to kiss him. It was the oldest trick in the book: pretend to be lovers to mislead anyone who was looking for one person, not two. He was almost disappointed she would resort to it.

The rest of him waited for it, remembering just how long it had been since he'd had a woman. His self-imposed solitude had had one major drawback.

It never happened.

She caught him off guard—again. She came close enough that it would look like they were kissing, but far enough that they weren't. They were enclosed in almost complete darkness, isolated in a cocoon of night. He could only see her eyes. They stared up at him, beseeching, pleading with him not to pull away, not to make a sound, not to reveal their position.

Ross didn't move.

It wasn't because of her silent plea. It was because, even now, moments later, the sound of her voice echoed in his ears.

Her accent was straight out of the Bronx, if his ear wasn't too rusty. And he knew, in a flash of knowledge so instinctive he didn't dare question it, that this was the person Roy Taylor was looking for.

Taylor was the man chasing her.

Immediately the events of the past few minutes began to shift in Ross's mind, realigning themselves, taking on new, complicated meanings. Suddenly the warm, pliant and frightened woman in his arms was no longer a casual stranger, but someone who had real importance in his life.

If she was running from Taylor, she had reason to be afraid. More than one.

At last someone burst out of the alley and skidded to a halt. Then came a muffled curse, the sound offering the confirmation he needed. He knew that voice.

Taylor.

He must have stiffened in spite of himself, the need to go after the man that keyed into his system. Taylor was just a few feet away, right behind him. He didn't know Ross was there. All Ross had to do was turn around and he had him.

The woman's hands tightened in his hair, not enough to hurt but more than enough to let him know she didn't intend to let him go.

It was the only reminder he needed. Ross stayed where he was, peering down at the woman in the dark. Though he never would have believed it, he had something more important than Taylor. He had something Taylor wanted. And something Taylor was willing to jump bail to pursue had to be very important indeed.

Though she made no sound, her chest rose and fell in a ragged pattern, causing her breasts to rub against his body in an unconsciously erotic fashion. In spite of himself, he felt his groin tighten.

Only the hard-won self-control forged after so many years

kept him from moving. He remained pinned against her, feeling every inch of her body pressed against his, her soft, sweet breath brushing his face, until he forgot everything— Taylor, Chastain, everything. There was nothing but him and this woman, a stranger who'd suddenly taken on a vast importance in his life.

He didn't even know her name.

It wasn't until it began to rain, fat, wet drops falling heavily on his head, that reality returned. Clarity came, as rude an awakening as the rain.

"Is he gone?"

Her voice contained the slightest tremor. He wasn't sure of the cause—him or Taylor. Not that it mattered.

He listened carefully, hearing nothing but the patter of rain on the pavement and the echo of thunder in the distance. When he finally pushed away from her, her fingers loosening their hold, the back of his head was drenched.

"Is he gone?" she asked again. She dropped her hands but couldn't move away. He literally had her up against a wall.

"I think so."

She nodded quickly, pursing her lips and dropping her head. He could see she was just beginning to notice how vulnerable her position was. There was a distinct wariness in her eyes now. No doubt she was beginning to wonder who the man was she'd just pressed herself against in a darkened street corner, trusting he was less of a danger than the one she was fleeing. Now she had to be wondering whether he was truly a lesser danger.

It was a good question. He doubted she would like the answer.

The light slanted over his shoulders, falling on her face. She had delicate features, perfectly carved with high cheekbones and a pert little nose, but there was nothing soft about her face. Tension gave her jaw an obstinate jut and made her expression hard as stone.

She was no innocent, that was for sure. The rashness of her actions and the cool resolve in her eyes told him that. Everything about her screamed guilt. He didn't have to know she was involved with Taylor to know she was in this up to her eyeballs. Which meant he had to proceed very carefully.

"Could you give me some air?" she said, shoving against his chest.

He relented, granting her a modicum of space by taking a step back. Enough to let her feel that he was no longer invading her space, not nearly enough for her to try to run.

"You want to tell me what that was about?" he asked.

The eyes that lifted to meet his were utterly blank, revealing nothing. "Just someone I didn't want to run into, that's all."

"Someone who scares you to death?" She blinked, startled. "Yeah, I noticed. That guy had you terrified."

She waved a hand. "Look, don't worry about it. I appreciate your help, but you're better off not getting involved. Trust me."

"In case you didn't notice, I'm already involved. You made sure I was."

Annoyance twisted her mouth. "Then I apologize for taking up three valuable minutes of your time. I'll let you get back to your life."

"I'm not going anywhere until I get some answers."

"What are you? A cop?" Though he couldn't miss the sarcastic edge, he also heard the uneasy note in her voice.

"No, I'm not a cop. But that's not a bad idea. If you don't want to tell me, you can tell the police."

Even in the dim light, he could see her go pale. Exactly as he expected.

He feigned surprise. "You were planning on reporting this, weren't you?" He didn't bother to keep the sarcastic edge from his words.

Not that she noticed. He could see her thinking quickly. Her tongue darted out to moisten parched lips, the motion betraying her tension.

It also captured his attention, drawing his gaze to her mouth. Her lips retained a sheen of wetness that made them shine.

Now those lips quivered. "Look, there's no reason to bring the cops into this. It's a personal matter. I can take care of it myself."

"With a little help from strangers?"

One eyebrow shot up. "I don't think I'll make that mistake again."

He might have been amused if the situation wasn't so dire. He was losing her, and whatever he did, he couldn't risk that. Two minutes ago he would have given anything to get his hands on Taylor. Now he had someone he suspected was more important, whoever she was. He'd haul her back to his truck if he wasn't sure she'd make a scene and bring Taylor back. One woman he could handle. A woman and Taylor— that would be tricky.

Taylor could be out there now, about to double back and find them. They didn't have time for this.

Twisting his features into something a little less forbidding, he said, "Look, at least let me walk you home. It's not safe for a woman to walk alone at night in a neighborhood like this."

She wanted to say no. He could read it in every inch of her expression and the rigid lines of her posture. But he doubted she could think of a good reason to say no that wouldn't arouse his suspicions more. He was counting on it.

And still she hesitated.

He kept his expression neutral, even as he felt the seconds tick by as steadily as the pulse throbbing at his neck.

"You really want to stand here arguing? Your friend could still be out there," he reminded her softly.

She searched his face again. He recognized the exact instant she made her decision. Her jaw tightened and the corners of her lips gave a violent twist as she pursed her mouth.

"Fine," she said. "Let's go."

With that, she spun out of his grasp and hurried back down the alley she'd first emerged from.

Allowing himself one small, satisfied smile, Ross fell into step behind her and followed her into the darkness.

PRICE CHASTAIN rolled off of the woman beneath him and jerked their tangled limbs apart. She gave a little gasp of shock—either not finished herself or not finished faking it. The sound barely pierced his concentration. Swinging his legs over the side of the bed, he checked the clock on the nightstand. It was well after midnight. He should have heard something by now.

She laid her hand on his bare back. "What's the matter?" she murmured, running her hand across his shoulders. "You were barely with me there."

He shrugged off her touch. The contact was making his skin crawl. "Get out. I have business to take care of."

If she was annoyed by his tone, she didn't show it. Smart girl. The mattress sagged as she climbed off the bed. He didn't bother to look as she padded naked to the bathroom.

As soon as she was gone, Chastain rolled his shoulders to shake off the lingering sensation of her sweaty palms and twisted his neck until he felt that satisfying crack. Mariana was a great lay, but lately she was starting to ask questions, nothing dangerous, certainly nothing about what she had to be hearing in the news, but little things. She was starting to get clingy. He was going to have to get rid of her soon.

He hated women who asked questions. That was exactly how he'd found himself in his current situation.

He checked the clock again. Less than a minute had passed.

The phone remained silent.

Taylor had told him the woman got off work at eleven CST. He should have her by now.

Something had gone wrong.

He grabbed the phone and hit the speed dial for Taylor's cell. Taylor picked up on the fourth ring. "Hello?"

"It's me."

Taylor's silence buzzed across the line.

"Well? Do you have her?" Chastain couldn't even bring himself to say her name.

A few more seconds of silence, followed by a reluctant "No."

Chastain gripped the receiver so tightly his hand went numb. "No?"

"I lost her."

He nearly hurled the phone across the room. "What do you mean, you lost her? You assured me the situation was under control."

"She must have figured something was up. She bolted."

"She can't have gotten far. Find her."

"I will. Don't worry about it. She's not getting away."

"You'd damn well better hope she doesn't. I want to hear back that you've got her within the hour."

He slammed the phone down, cutting off the rest of Taylor's useless assurances. He hated having to rely on the overgrown Neanderthal, but Taylor was the only person he could trust, the only one with as much on the line as Chastain himself.

Unable to sit still any longer, he climbed to his feet and crossed to the ceiling-to-floor windows with their flawless view of Central Park. The sight did little to calm him. He had people paying him millions for a view like this. He owned half the city, and he stood to lose it all. There were a lot of people who'd love to see it happen. The D.A. was looking to score political points. The cops would be lining up to see him go down. And every property owner and tenant he'd had to coax cooperation from in the past would be falling over themselves with glee.

He felt like throwing open the windows and screaming at every one of them that it wasn't going to happen. He hadn't worked for everything he'd built to lose it all now.

It wasn't going to happen. His reflection stared back at him in the glass. His gaze was clear and determined, the sign of a man who knew his own path and always had. Price Chastain made his own destiny, just like he'd made his own name. His destiny was to always come out on top.

That wasn't about to change.

RETURNING HIS CELL PHONE to the clip on his belt, Roy Taylor scanned the empty street for any sign of the woman. He gritted his teeth, grinding his molars together so hard he felt a jolt of pain shoot along his jaw. The action was the only outlet he gave to the fury simmering in his veins.

It was bad enough the woman had managed to escape. He didn't need Chastain riding him about it. As if he didn't have as much to lose as Chastain did if they didn't get their hands on her before anyone else did.

He shouldn't have answered the phone. Except he knew Chastain would just keep calling back until he did.

The twenty calls a day he was fielding from the man told him everything he needed to know. Chastain didn't trust him. He thought he was going to take off and leave him holding the bag. Well, Roy Taylor was no coward. He wasn't about to spend the rest of his life running.

Eight years of picking up after the man, and Chastain acted like he'd never done a thing for him. Taylor sure wasn't the one who'd screwed everything up. Chastain had done it all by himself and now they were all paying for it.

Taylor picked up his pace, heading back in the direction he was sure the woman had gone. He was going to find her, all right. It was what he always did. He got the job done, no matter what it took.

But not for Chastain this time. For himself.

Chastain could think whatever the hell he wanted. The only person Roy Taylor was looking out for was Roy Taylor.

It was every man for himself.

Chapter Three

She did her best to ignore him as they wound their way through the back alleys that led to her apartment. There was a faster, more direct route of course, but she wasn't about to risk running into Taylor on one of those streets.

Already she was plotting her next move for when she reached her apartment and ditched her unwanted companion. She'd memorized the bus schedules out of Chicago her first day in the city. Her bag was packed. All she needed to do was pick it up, and she could catch the "EL" back to the bus station. She should be on her way to parts unknown before dawn. The destination would be wherever the first bus out of town took her. It was pretty straightforward.

She picked up the pace, ready to be on her way. The man behind her didn't miss a step. She frowned in annoyance. Of all the times to pick up a Good Samaritan.

She didn't even know what he looked like, she realized. His face had remained in shadow back on the corner. All she knew was that he was tall and strong. The man was muscular as hell, and she'd been pressed up against every one of those muscles.

She wondered idly what she was doing. It wasn't like it mattered how built the guy was. After the next couple of minutes, she was never going to see him again.

He didn't say a word to her until they reached the run-down five-story building she'd called home for the past four months. She plowed up the steps without looking back at him, but sensed him appraising the structure.

"Nice place," he said in a tone dry as dust.

"It's a dump. You can say it." The observation wouldn't offend her. She hadn't exactly been focusing on the building's aesthetic qualities when it had come to finding a place to live.

She pushed the front door open, and when she didn't immediately sense him behind her, she thought for a second he was going to leave. The notion was crushed an instant later when he laid his hand on the door and held it open for her. Rather than chance Taylor coming across them on the front stoop, she plunged inside and let him follow. She'd have to save the goodbyes for her front door. Like it or not, he would be saying goodbye then.

"Aren't you worried he'll follow you here?" her Samaritan asked as he trailed her up the unlit stairs.

"No. He doesn't know about the apartment." If he had he would have waited to ambush her here. Instead, he'd come after her in a public place.

"So it wasn't random."

Had she revealed too much? Too late to worry about it now. "No. It wasn't random."

She finally reached the third floor. Her apartment was the first on the left, facing the front of the building. Key already in hand, she shoved it into the lock, threw the door open and whirled back to face him before he'd stepped onto the shadowy landing.

"See. I made it. Safe and sound."

Looming over her, he looked past her into the apartment. She doubted he could see much. It was still probably enough to let him know it wasn't any more hospitable than the rest of the structure. Or the woman who lived there. "Lady, I'm not sure I feel safe in this building."

"Then you're welcome to leave."

He made no move to do so. He stared at her, long and hard, until her skin began to tingle in response. She shifted uneasily from one foot to the other, doing her best not to rub at the goose bumps.

"I don't think you feel safe here, either."

"I'll be fine. I've been here for quite a while. Nothing's happened to me yet."

"Because Taylor didn't know where you were until today."

The words were so unexpected she couldn't hide her reaction. He might as well have punched her. The air whooshed from her lungs, the blood from her face.

She knew immediately she'd made a mistake.

She hurried to cover for it. "I don't know what you're talking about."

He moved closer, every bit as big and intimidating as he'd been on the street. She managed to hold her ground.

He planted a hand on the door to keep her from slamming it in his face. A thought that hadn't even occurred to her, she realized. Damn it. She had to get her head together.

"Nice try, lady. But I'm well acquainted with Roy Taylor. I know the sound of his voice as well as my own, and I know he's the man you were trying to get away from back there. Just like I know you're a native New Yorker."

Oh, God. He *was* with Taylor.

And she'd led him straight into her home.

The surprise passed quickly, replaced by the anger she knew so well.

She channeled every bit of it into a glare that should have had him stepping back. "I don't know anybody named Trainer."

"Taylor."

"Whatever. And I'm from Chicago. Born and bred right here on the South Side. Go Sox." She made sure every word dripped with the distinctive accent she'd learned to affect early on. There could be no doubt where she was from.

She couldn't see it, but she could sense him smile. "You let your accent slip back there in the street. You've got it back now. Pretty good, I have to admit. I never would have guessed."

Was he telling the truth? It was certainly possible. She'd been half out of her mind back there.

He took advantage of her momentary silence to step forward again, forcing her to retreat just enough for him to step inside and shut the door behind him. Not bothering with the lock, he reached over and flipped on the light.

The glow from the single yellow bulb wasn't enough of a shock that her eyes needed time to adjust. The light flared and then there he was, exposed to her for the first time.

He was just as intimidating in the light as he'd been in the dark. His face matched his body. Shaggy black hair crowned a head composed of sharp features and hard angles. He was older than she'd imagined for some reason, maybe forty. Lines were carved into thick grooves around his eyes and mouth. He wasn't a man anyone would describe as handsome. He was too hard. Too cold. Too purely masculine in a raw, elemental way. Unyielding. Dangerous.

She found her voice at last. "Who are you?"

"The name's Ross. I'm a bounty hunter."

"I hate to break it to you, Ross, but there's no bounty out on me."

"I'm not after you. I'm after Taylor."

A bounty hunter. She almost laughed out loud. All the people who were after her, and the one who'd caught her was looking for someone else. He'd found a lot more than he'd bargained for and had no idea what he had.

"Your turn," he said. "Who are you?"

"That's none of your business."

He grabbed her arm before she could move, his fingers digging through the layers of clothes. "Lady, anything and everything related to Roy Taylor is my business. That makes you my business."

She didn't even blink. He'd lost the ability to shock her after that last bombshell. "No," she said quietly, forcefully, looking him straight in the eye with one arched brow. She jerked out of his grasp. "It doesn't."

She noted with some satisfaction the hint of frustration that entered those pale gray eyes. It was quickly replaced by a far less-encouraging hard determination.

One corner of his mouth curved in challenge. "Then you won't mind if I call the police and report what happened tonight."

The police. Her heart lurched in her chest at the notion. If there was anyone more dangerous to her than Taylor, it was them.

"I don't have a phone."

He reached into the inside pocket of his jacket. "I do."

She kept her expression impassive. "Do what you want. I'm going to go change."

Then she was moving again, quickly, before he had a chance to react. She dodged into the bedroom a few feet away—the benefit of living in an apartment roughly the size of a postage stamp—and slammed the door shut behind her. The lock on the door wouldn't give him much trouble if he tried coming after her. She flipped it, anyway, willing to take what she could get.

She was across the room in a flash. Her backpack was sitting on the mattress where she'd left it. Thankfully she hadn't set it by the front door like she'd originally planned. Grabbing it, she moved to the bedroom window. It slid up silently at her touch. She created enough of an opening to fit through, then tossed her backpack through it, following a second later.

She landed hard on her hands and knees on the cold metal of the fire escape. It swayed beneath her. She ignored the motion—there was no time to be afraid of anything but the man who'd be coming after her at any moment—slung the backpack over her shoulder and hurried down the fire escape. With each step, it felt like she was moving too slow. Her feet kept slipping on the framework, her hands struggled to find purchase every time she fell. There were only three flights down to the street. It might as well have been a hundred. She glanced down and all she saw was darkness.

Fear lodged in her throat. She swallowed it back with the same ruthlessness with which she'd done everything so far. She couldn't give in to fear. There was no time for it.

She finally reached the end. She'd have to jump the rest of the way. She dropped her backpack over the ledge, using the sound of its landing to judge the distance to the ground. A few feet. She could make that. She had to.

The landing jarred every bone in her body. It hurt, but not enough to signal anything was broken. Even before her body stopped weaving in an attempt to steady itself, she grabbed for the backpack, threw it over her shoulder and plunged forward into the night.

Two steps later she ran into a wall. Again.

An iron hand clamped down on her forearm. She jerked her head up in shock to face the man who loomed over her. Her first thought was that it had to be Ross, but then she realized it wasn't. This man wasn't quite as tall or broad. The uneasy sensation that skittered along her nerve endings warned her he was infinitely more dangerous.

"Gotcha," he sneered, and her alarm skyrocketed.

"I don't think so."

The familiar voice came from behind her, startling both her and her captor. Almost as the words were spoken, she was yanked out of his grasp. He barely had time to lift his head before a fist came out of the darkness and landed a blow to the chin that sent him crashing to the ground.

Her savior spun her around to face him. She looked up in shock to meet Ross's steely glare.

"How—"

"Back door," he said, his voice grave. "There's something you need to understand. I'm not stupid."

His tone revived her anger. "You have to be. A smarter man would take a hint." She dropped her gaze to the hand fastened to her arm like a vise. "If you want to keep that hand, I suggest you remove it."

"Fine." She was so surprised by his capitulation she didn't even realize what he was doing until he had the cuff fastened around her wrist.

Outraged, she jerked at the metal ring affixing her arm to his. "Get this off me!"

"Do you really want to argue about this now?"

As if on cue, the man at their feet let out a soft groan.

Ross arched a brow at her. "Another friend of yours?"

She shook her head. "I don't know who he is."

"Well, we can wait for your new friend here to wake up and see what he has to say about it. Or maybe we should wait for Taylor to show up."

"I told you I don't know any Taylor."

"And I told you I don't believe you. Take your pick, lady. Taylor or me."

She scrambled for another option and came up empty. She just knew she didn't want to stand there arguing with him. Like it or not, Taylor *was* out there. "Fine," she said through gritted teeth. "Let's get out of here."

She moved first to take the lead. Ross didn't give her the

chance. He surged forward toward the rear of the building, pulling her with him.

He stopped at the back of the building to make sure it was clear. Once he'd ascertained it was, he started moving again without saying a word. There was nothing for her to do but follow.

For now.

THE SEDAN had New York plates.

Taylor barely glimpsed the license plate out of the corner of his eye. He was halfway down the block when the fact sank in.

After a half hour of aimlessly wandering the streets, he'd doubled back to the main one where the bar and the drugstore where the woman worked were located. Being on foot was getting him nowhere. He could cover more ground in his car.

But he'd kept alert on his way back, searching for any sign of the woman, paying attention to everything that fell within his range of vision.

Like the sedan with New York plates.

Curious, he turned around and narrowed his eyes on the car parked along the curb. He'd passed a pickup truck with New York plates farther down the block. Then the sedan. And of course his own vehicle was waiting around the corner.

Now what were the chances that three vehicles from New York would all be here tonight without being connected?

It was possible. There had to be millions of cars registered with New York State, all with corresponding plates.

But Taylor didn't believe in coincidences.

Before he had a chance to consider it further, a man appeared down the street pulling a woman with him. Both quickly looked around them, neither seeing him tucked away in the shadows down the block. They quickly made their way to a truck parked along the curb. The truck he'd noted with New York plates.

He had no trouble recognizing the woman, despite the change in her hair from a year ago. It was the sight of the man that blindsided him.

His mouth curling into a sneer, Taylor bit back a curse. Gideon Ross. The two-bit bounty hunter had been a pain in his ass for too long, ever since the death of that washed-up old man. Taylor had thought he'd been rid of the bastard when he finally left the city.

And now he had the woman.

Damn it. It was all he could do not to grab his weapon from his shoulder holster and take aim. He and Chastain had always known how bad it would be if anyone else got their hands on her before Taylor did. But for Ross to be the one might just be the worst-case scenario.

Taylor took an instinctive step forward, then quickly stepped back into the shadows and considered his options. He could hustle down the block and try to get to the truck before they left, but he probably wouldn't be able to stop them. Or he could run back to his own vehicle and try to follow. They'd likely be long gone before he got back.

Almost absently, he dropped his hand into his pocket and pulled out the tracking device he'd been fooling around with for a while now. He'd thought it might come in handy if she managed to hop on a bus or grab a cab before he could stop her. The only problem was he was nowhere near close enough to get the transmitter on the truck, and there was little chance he could do so before they took off.

Down the block, Ross pushed the woman into the passenger side of the truck, but not before she elbowed him in the ribs. Even from a distance, Taylor could tell it had to hurt. Obviously the woman was not going willingly. He took no satisfaction from the knowledge.

By the time the truck roared to life and pulled away from the curb, he knew he had no choice but to get back to his car and try to catch them before they got too far.

Just as he started to turn away, a man rushed out of an alley up ahead, coming from the same direction Ross and the woman had.

Taylor froze, his gut telling him not to move just yet. Maybe Ross and the woman hadn't just been running. Maybe they'd been running *from* something. Or somebody.

Maybe somebody else from New York?

Without even thinking about it, he used his thumb to flip a tiny switch on the back of the tracking device. It didn't make a sound. It didn't need to. He knew the transmitter was activated.

His attention shifted to the sedan parked down the block. The other vehicle with New York plates. Sure enough, the man was quickly striding in that direction.

But who was this guy? Someone else after the woman?

The questions could wait. Instinct told him he couldn't risk losing this guy.

Taylor darted through the shadows toward the vehicle. The other man made his way down the sidewalk, only crossing when he reached the car. Taylor made it there first and waited, hidden in a darkened storefront doorway. The man had no idea he was there.

When the man climbed into his car, Taylor made his move. He shot out at the exact moment the car door slammed shut and fell to his stomach on the pavement behind the car. As the engine rumbled to life, he reached up and shoved the transmitter under the back bumper.

The car started to pull away. Taylor pushed off on his elbows and shoved himself backward—right under the parked car behind him.

He lay there, immobile, and listened to the car disappearing into the night. A good minute passed before it was gone and the street was silent again.

Only then did he roll out from under the other car. Rising to his feet, he didn't so much as brush himself off as he crossed the street and headed back to where he'd parked his own set of wheels.

The chase was back on.

Chapter Four

They crossed the state line into Indiana a little after one in the morning. By then, they'd driven out of one storm and into the one that had passed through Chicago earlier that day. Driving sheets of rain battered the truck, creating a roar that surrounded them on all sides. The effect only heightened the silence that crackled between Ross and the woman.

All things considered, Ross thought he'd done pretty well. He didn't have Taylor, true, but he had something Taylor wanted, and that had to be a lot more valuable.

The only question was, what exactly did he have?

Ross resisted the urge to glance at her out of the corner of his eye. She was braced against the passenger door, her wrist shackled to a metal bar bolted to the dashboard. He'd locked her in before she knew what he was doing as soon as they reached the vehicle. She hadn't looked at him since, her attention stubbornly focused outside her window.

Ross rubbed at the tension knotting the back of his neck. He'd taken in female skips before, enough that he should have known how to expect a cornered woman to behave. Usually by this point, when they had a chance to realize they weren't going to get away from him, they reacted by either screaming or bursting into tears, as if a show of emotion could sway him into letting them go. Most included a sob story, some yarn about how they were framed or justified or otherwise blameless, little realizing he'd heard their story before in a million other forms, and no teary eyes or wobbly lips were going to make it any more believable this time around.

This woman did none of that. She sat there against the door, her free hand lying in her lap, and looked resolutely away. She said nothing. If it wasn't for her ramrod posture and her too-studious show of nonchalance, he might have actually believed she'd managed to forget about him.

Under normal circumstances, he might have appreciated the peace and quiet. Instead, it made him uneasy. It meant she was thinking, planning her inevitable escape attempt, no doubt. He would have to put an end to that. He was too tired to put up with any more of her nonsense tonight. He could already feel a bruise forming where she'd elbowed him in the ribs before stepping into the truck.

He grimaced at the soreness. He didn't used to be so delicate. *Too old, man. You're too damn old for this crap.*

He cleared his throat. "You planning on saying anything on this trip?"

She didn't move a muscle, didn't even glance his way. "What do you want? A hissy fit?"

He'd like that a lot more than what she was giving him. He knew how to deal with screamers. "I'll settle for a name."

"Connie Baker."

She said it so easily he might have believed her under different circumstances. "Nice try. What is it really?"

She finally looked at him then. She said nothing.

"Like you'd really tell me that easy."

She shrugged one shoulder and turned her face away from him.

"We should talk about what happened back there."

"Why?"

"Because if we're going to be running into trouble, I could use the advance warning."

Her snort said exactly what she thought of that idea. "You expect me to help you in this kidnapping?"

"I haven't kidnapped you."

She rattled the handcuff. "What do you call this?"

"Consider yourself in custody."

"I haven't done anything."

"Then you won't mind if I check that with the police."

She glowered at him from beneath hooded lids. Her pupils sparked pure malice from the tiny slits.

"I didn't think so."

"What are you going to check with the police? You don't even know my name."

"They can run your prints."

"They're not on file. I told you, I'm not a criminal."

He managed not to smile. *That's it. Keep talking.* Soon she'd tell him all he needed to know without realizing she was doing it.

"If you have knowledge that could impact Chastain's trial and you're not coming forward with it, you might as well be."

"Might as well be. Doesn't mean I am."

"Innocent people don't run."

Her laugh caught him off guard. The sound was bitter, humorless. "Sometimes that's all you can do."

There was something so hopeless in the statement that Ross felt himself respond to it. He pushed the feeling away, refusing to be taken in. She was good. He'd known that. He just hadn't figured how good.

"If you're going for pity, you're going to have to do better than that."

He met her eyes briefly. There was no anger or guile there. Just blank coldness. "I'm not looking for anything from you.

But if you take me to the police, you'll be signing my death warrant."

"Try singing a song I haven't heard before."

He'd expected anger. Still there wasn't a flicker of emotion in her stare. "Why did you want me to talk if you're not interested in anything I have to say?"

"Fine. You're in trouble. I got that. If you're involved with Chastain it's no wonder."

She cocked her head and really looked at him, as though seeing something for the first time. "You hate him."

"Yeah, I do."

"So do I."

"Great. We have something in common. If we're going to be best friends, you mind telling me your name?"

"You first. Your full name."

"Gideon Ross. I'm a bounty hunter. I'm after Taylor. That's all you need to know."

"Then why don't you go after him and leave me alone?"

"Because he's after you, and I want to know why."

"Does it matter?"

"It sure as hell does. He jumped bail to come after you. There has to be a good reason. If it has anything to do with the trial, I intend to find out."

"It doesn't," she said quickly. Too quickly.

"You might want to give the truth a try. You're a lousy liar."

"I'm not telling you anything."

"Suit yourself. I'm not in that much of a hurry. We've got plenty of road ahead of us."

"Where are *we* going?"

The answer came automatically. The place he had to get her if she could have an impact on Chastain's trial. "New York."

"No!"

She almost lunged out of her seat and grabbed the wheel away from him. He had no doubt that if it wasn't for the cuffs holding her in place, she would have done just that. As it was, the metal chain nearly snapped as she jerked her arm toward him, only to be flung back against the seat.

She crouched there like a caged animal, chest heaving. "I can't go back to New York. They'll kill me."

Whatever else she was lying about, it was clear she believed that. He tried to strike a reassuring note. It wasn't exactly his specialty. "Nothing's going to happen to you while you're with me. Consider this protective custody."

"Right." She dragged the word out to several syllables, every one dripping with disdain. "I'm supposed to trust you?"

"You don't have a choice."

The dim glow of a motel sign gravitated closer in the darkness. Ross eased off the gas.

"But for now, we're going to get a room for the night. I need the sleep. I'm guessing you do, too."

She didn't say anything. He didn't mind this time. Talking was getting them nowhere. He had plenty of time to get the truth out of her. It was a long drive back to New York.

Only when he pulled into the gravel driveway of the Rest-a-W-ile Motel—a burnt-out letter *H* presumably in there somewhere—did she speak.

"You should know that I'm going to fight you every step of the way."

Ross smiled drily and met her cold stare head-on. "In case you didn't notice, lady, you already are."

THE ROOM HE BOOKED for them was at the very end of the motel, the better to keep anyone from interceding when he dragged her there by the cuffs, she guessed. It was out of sight of the office and no one was around when they tromped through the rain to it.

The place looked so bleak from the outside she couldn't

imagine the inside could be any worse. That was before she got her first look at the orange interior that was either fading into brown or so covered in grime the real color was masked, and the twin beds, one of which was missing a leg and leaning at a downward slant on one side. Only someone with an affinity for cockroaches and the stink of cigarettes would even think of resting here a w-ile.

"And I thought my place was a dump."

"Beggars can't be choosers," Ross said beside her.

"I don't remember begging for any part of this. And while we're at it, do you have any more clichés you'd like to get off your chest?"

He locked the door behind them. "I'll let you know."

"You do that." She gave the handcuffs a yank and pulled away from him. "I'm going to take a shower."

"All right." He walked over to the bathroom, dragging her all the way. He shoved the door open with one toe and snapped the light on, giving the room a perfunctory once-over. He turned back to her. "All clear."

"Except for the cockroaches."

One corner of his mouth tilted upward for a fraction of a second. "Thought I'd be a nice guy and not mention that."

"You haven't bothered being nice up to this point. Why start now?"

"Good point."

Fuming, she held out her wrists. "Aren't you going to take these off?"

He surveyed her for a long moment. She stared right back, never blinking. Finally he produced the key and unlocked the cuffs.

Rubbing her wrists, she grabbed her backpack and spun away from him toward the bathroom.

"Aren't you going to say thank-you?"

"What do you think?" she said over her shoulder.

She took two steps toward the bathroom before he stopped her.

"Take your clothes off before you go into the bathroom."

Her first instinct was to ignore him and keep walking. Intuition told her she'd never make it.

She turned around slowly. "Excuse me?"

He stood where she'd left him with his arms folded across his chest. Cold. Unrelenting. His tone and expression allowed no argument.

"You want a shower, you leave everything out here."

"Why?"

One brow shot up, mocking her. "Why do you think? Your bag and your clothes stay out here."

She thought fast. "Fine. Turn around."

"Not a chance. I've put up with enough from you tonight without adding a blow to the back of the head to it."

"I am not taking my clothes off in front of you."

"Suit yourself. Doesn't make a difference to me one way or the other if you get a shower. I'd just as soon get some sleep. Pick your bed and we'll call it a night."

"I bet you're not even a bounty hunter. You're probably just a crazy perv who dragged me here to get me naked."

"Lady, I don't care if you're Playmate of the Year. You want to keep your clothes on, fine. It's up to you."

"Really did change your mind about that whole being-nice thing, didn't you?"

"I told you. I'm not stupid."

She let a sigh whistle through her teeth. She was too tired to argue about this. She was soaked through and freezing. Even if she wouldn't kill for a shower right about now, she needed to change. Her feet still throbbed from standing on them all day, her back was killing her, her wrists hurt from the handcuffs. All she wanted was ten minutes under the stinging spray of a showerhead with decent water pressure, and Gideon Ross—a phony name if ever she'd heard one, and she should know—be damned. At this point she'd probably be willing to do a striptease for Price Chastain himself if that was what it took.

But she wasn't about to let this guy see her naked. A tremor shuddered through her. She couldn't.

They stared at each other. Neither blinked. He simply continued to watch her, his eyes never wavering from hers, no expression whatsoever on his face. Waiting. He would put her through this and it didn't matter to him either way.

It was that damn impassiveness that drove away her apprehension, leaving anger in its place. She let it build. Anger, she knew what to do with.

He really didn't care. Deep down she didn't think he would attack her. He might be a big jerk, but something told her he wasn't that kind of guy. He was too self-righteous. He didn't care about her body. He didn't care about her. All he wanted was Taylor, and he had no problem using her to get to him, as if that wasn't even worse than anything he could do to her body. He would put her through hell and risk her life if it meant getting what he wanted.

But he wouldn't touch her.

She knew exactly how she could use that to her advantage. "Fine."

She saw the flash of surprise in his eyes as she dropped the bag onto the floor. It was the only reaction he gave her.

She threw her head back in defiance and jerked the coat from her shoulders. Glaring straight into his eyes, she whipped it at his feet.

"All right, Ross. Is this what you want? Do you want to see everything?"

He frowned. "Look, lady—"

"No. Tell me how you want it." She kicked off her shoes,

sending them flying across the room. One almost hit him in the leg. He didn't even flinch.

"Do you want it fast?" She stabbed the heel of one foot into the toe of the opposite sock and yanked it off. "Or slow?" She repeated the motion with other foot, putting a little wiggle in her hips.

"Do you like that?" The words were suggestive, but she couldn't keep the anger out of her voice. "Should I do a little dance? Is that what you want? A striptease?"

"Knock it off." There was a dangerous edge in his tone. She allowed herself to feel the tiniest bit of satisfaction. She was starting to get to him.

"Why? Isn't this what you want?"

"No."

"Really?" She reached for the hem of her shirt. He never lowered his gaze from her face. She could still tell he knew exactly what she was doing.

She started to lift it over her stomach. "What about this? Is this better?"

"Lady…" The word came out like a growl.

She froze as though reconsidering, and released the shirt, reaching for the button on her pants, instead. "Or maybe you're the kind of guy who wants to get right to the good stuff. Is that it?" She popped the button and slid the zipper down, the rasp loud in the silence of the room. She began to shift her hips from side to side, shimmying out of the slacks. They slid down her thighs and pooled at her feet. Cold air washed over her bare legs. She felt just how exposed she was. Embarrassed heat flooded her skin. She knew her face had gone red.

She forced herself to step out of the pants, bringing her one step closer to him. His face had gone red, too. Not with embarrassment, though. With anger.

"How's this, Ross?" Her voice shook for the first time. She

would have given anything for him to think it was out of anger. Even to her own ears it sounded like fear. But she never looked away from him, never lowered her head one bit. "Do you like this? Am I getting it right?"

His body had gone so rigid he looked as taut as piano wire and just as ready to snap. "I don't know what kind of game you're playing, but that's enough."

"It's your game, bounty hunter." She hooked her thumbs into her panties. She couldn't tell if it was her hands or her torso that was shaking. Or both. "You're the one who wanted a look, aren't you? You're the one who wanted to see exactly what you've got your hands on—"

He was across the room in a heartbeat before she knew what was happening. For one terrifying moment, she knew she'd pushed him too far. He was in her face, grabbing her by both shoulders, practically lifting her off the ground. His fingers dug into her skin so hard she winced. He towered over her, huge and strong and frightening. She couldn't breathe. She couldn't do anything but stare up into his eyes and wait to see what he would do next.

His anger crackled around him like static electricity. She could almost feel it jolt through her where he touched her. The shock of his fingers on her bare skin held her immobile. He was so close she could smell him, the dampness from the rain and a distinctively masculine musk. His fingers tightened on her shoulders and she couldn't stop the little gasp that flew out of her mouth.

The sound seemed to penetrate his fury. He relaxed his hold and released her, taking a step back. She rocked back on her heels, unsteady on her feet. The anger didn't ease from his features. He didn't take his eyes off her face.

When he spoke, his voice was tight. "I told you. That's not what I want."

I know. She couldn't explain why she had the urge to reassure him. Or the sudden spurt of disappointment that rose inside her.

Somehow she managed to find her voice. "And what *do* you want?"

"Not that. I told you nothing would happen to you while you're with me."

"Because you've done everything to make me think I can trust you up till now, right, Ross?"

"I promise you. I will not let anything happen to you."

He meant it. She could hear the conviction in every word. That made them hurt that much more. She felt them like physical blows.

She couldn't look at him anymore, couldn't take his sincerity. She knew better than to depend on it. She knew it couldn't last.

She lowered her head. "You shouldn't make promises you can't keep."

She felt him give her one long, assessing look, then turn away from her. "Go into the bathroom," he said.

She didn't reach for her bag or her clothes. All she wanted to do was retreat, to get away from this overpowering man and his sincerity and his promises before she let herself get sucked in. She stumbled toward the bathroom and the sanctuary it offered.

"I can't help you unless you let me."

She stopped in the doorway. The words were spoken softly. There was no trace of coercion, no impatience, no anger. Only a simple statement of truth. He couldn't help her unless she let him.

She slowly glanced back over her shoulder at him. He looked so big, so solid, even standing all the way across the room. The dim lighting masked his eyes from her, something that usually would have worried her. She'd learned to use people's eyes to gauge their honesty, their trustworthiness.

She could tell nothing about this man from where she stood. Only that he was big and broad and strong, seeming capable of warding off the entire world and keeping her safe.

For the briefest of moments, she was tempted. Boy, was she tempted. In that instant, she would have given anything to be able to trust him. All of a sudden, more than ever before, she realized just how tired she was. Tired of running, tired of looking over her shoulder everywhere she went. It didn't feel like she could make it another day, another hour, another minute. She'd been running for so long, fighting for so long, that she could barely remember a time when she wasn't. It was an infinite road with no end in sight. She wasn't sure she could do it anymore.

The offer was so tempting, the chance to hand her problems over to this man and have him save her. She would give anything to be able to trust someone, anyone, for the first time in so long, to turn her face into that wide chest, to ease her burden onto those shoulders and let someone else carry the load, if only for a short time.

But trusting this man would be a mistake.

He was the enemy. How could she even think of forgetting that? It wasn't a coincidence that he'd appeared in her life just before all hell broke loose. He was tangled up in this as much as any of the men who were chasing her down, and twice as dangerous.

She didn't say a word. There was nothing she could say, nothing he would understand, that wouldn't require explanations she couldn't give. Instead, she turned away and escaped into the bathroom, the moment over. Reality had set in, offering the cold reminder that she couldn't trust this man or any other.

He was half-right.

He couldn't help her at all.

DAMN.

Ross watched the bathroom door close behind her and

swallowed a groan of frustration. For a second there, he thought she might tell him.

He was good at reading people, sensing a mood change from a muscle reflex or batted eye. He could have sworn he'd almost gotten to her. His gut said she was wavering, on the verge of coming clean.

And then she turned away without so much as a word.

A ragged breath worked its way from his lungs. His chest was so tight, he'd barely been able to breathe.

She was good, whoever she was. Damn good at making him feel like a jerk. He didn't like seeing women terrified of him. He could deal with the women who just didn't want to face what they had coming to them, scared of paying for what they'd done. That was one thing. But seeing this woman, shaking like a leaf, acting like he was about to attack her, like he *was* attacking her...that was something else.

She hadn't looked much different when he'd caught her running from Taylor. Now that was a comparison he wasn't comfortable with.

The worst part was knowing that he had looked. At that quick flash of stomach before she dropped the shirt. At every long inch of leg exposed below the edge of it. If she'd taken everything off, he damn well would have looked. He'd been angry when he stopped her, all right. Angry that he might turn out to be the bastard she said he was.

He still wasn't sure how much of that had been real and how much was an act. How much he should believe those big liquid eyes she'd aimed at him when he had her cornered. He knew she was a fighter and she'd rip out his throat given half a chance. How that gelled with the woman terrified of taking her clothes off in front of him, he didn't know. He wasn't sure he wanted to. He wanted to believe it was a sham.

Everything inside him told him it wasn't.

He heard her flip the lock on the bathroom door. She was

kidding herself if she thought that flimsy bolt could keep him out of there if he wanted in. With any luck, he wouldn't have to prove it to her.

He crossed the room in two strides to stand outside the door. He waited until he heard the water in the shower come on, and then, so soft he almost missed it, her moan as she stepped beneath the spray.

He listened to the water for a few seconds, the unmistakable sound of it pounding against flesh, rather than the uninterrupted impact of the spray against the tiles. She was in there, all right. From the sound of it, she would be for a while.

He could picture her there, all the parts he'd seen, his mind filling in all the rest. He didn't need to see everything. He'd felt most of it, pressed up against him in that alley. He could see it now, as clear as if he were in that room with her. Tilting her head back into the spray. Sliding her hands over her body. Over her breasts, her flat belly, and down low—

Damn it all. He shoved away from the door before he could break it down. He was the one who needed a shower. A cold one.

She was right. He was some crazy perv. With some effort, he pushed the image away. He didn't have time for this. He had to take advantage of this opportunity while he had the chance.

Without the slightest bit of guilt, he lifted her bag onto the nearest bed and began to pull out its contents. There were mostly clothes, rolled into haphazard balls to optimize space. Most of them were starting to look a little threadbare, well maintained but none of them anywhere close to being new. It made sense. Whatever money she had, she wouldn't be wasting it on clothes.

Tossing the clothes aside, he dug into the bottom of the bag and came up with a wallet and a wad of newspaper articles, all of them covering aspects of Chastain's trial. They went back several months. She'd been following the case closely. It wasn't exactly a surprise.

He heard something bouncing around the bottom of the backpack. Reaching in, his fingers closed around a hard rectangle of plastic. He felt a surge of triumph as he pulled it into the light.

It was three cards wedged together. A social security card stuck to the back of a credit card. And beneath them, a New York State driver's license. The solemn face pictured was unmistakable. The only new piece of information was the name.

Allie Freeman.

He smiled to himself. Now she had a name.

It wasn't one he was familiar with. He quickly memorized the address for when he called Newcomb. If she was involved with Chastain, then Newcomb had to know who she was.

Satisfied, he pocketed the cards. She wasn't going to need them since she wasn't going anywhere without him for a while.

The backpack emptied, Ross reached for the wallet he'd set aside. It held a number of bills, all fifties. He quickly flipped through them—650 bucks. Most likely all the money she had in the world. He left it where he'd found it. It was hers, and he wasn't going to take that from her. He'd been called a lot of things, but never a thief. At least not when it came to money, anyway.

There was no identification in the wallet, only the cash and a single photograph contained in the leather folds. It was faded from years of handling and curled around the edges. Gingerly he pried it from beneath the viewing window, leaving behind a latent imprint of the image on the plastic, and tilted it up to the light.

Three people were shown: a woman, a teenage girl and a

young boy. At least one stubborn face was familiar. It didn't take much deduction to figure out this was Allie's family.

Curious at this sole personal item contained in her belongings, Ross examined each face closely. The boy was grinning broadly, displaying a gap between his front teeth. Cute kid. He couldn't have been more than five or six, with a shaggy haircut and complete happiness shining from his features.

Ross felt a twinge in his chest as he stared at the kid's open smile. He'd almost forgotten that kind of innocence existed in the world. He couldn't remember ever being that happy. He couldn't even remember being five or six.

The kid's smile was almost painful to behold. For some reason Ross lingered over the image until it hurt too much to look at and he had to glance away.

The woman was smiling, too, though her expression showed more weariness than joy. It was the face of a woman who'd had her share of hard knocks. He couldn't guess her age. Her face was heavily lined, her smile hollow. He suspected she was far younger than she appeared. He would have said she was the kids' mother, though her face said grandmother.

The girl wasn't smiling. That was his Allie. But there was nothing amusing in this girl's expression. She looked older, too, and it had nothing to do with her physical appearance. There was a hardness to her, a less-pronounced version of the toughness she projected now. One hand rested on her brother's shoulder, the other on her mother's, the fingers tense. Though Ross knew it was probably a pose ordered by the photographer, there was something telling in the gesture. It was both protective and possessive, marking these two people as belonging to her.

"What the hell are you doing?"

Startled, Ross jerked his head up. The grown-up, flesh-and-blood version of the girl had opened the bathroom door and stepped into the room and he hadn't heard a thing. Now he couldn't help but notice her. Steam billowed behind her in a white cloud. She was wearing the shirt again, her legs bare.

For a second, his breath stuck in his throat.

There was nothing angelic about her expression. She looked on the verge of launching herself across the room.

"Were you going through my things?" She didn't give him a chance to answer before stalking across the room. "Give me that."

"Now hold on a minute—" He wasn't sure why he didn't release the photograph, why he held on to it just a fraction too long. It could have been that he was reacting to that contrary tone in her voice, the one that already had a way of getting his back up. But when she made a grab for the photograph, he didn't let go.

A second later the sound of paper tearing filled the room.

They both froze, staring down at the pieces of the photograph they each held. The top had been torn from the bottom, the girl cut off from the woman and boy.

Allie reached across and yanked the half he held out of his hand. This time, he had no trouble letting go. She blinked furiously, her eyes flickering everywhere but at him, her lips pressed into a tight line. Jerking away, she threw the photograph halves on the bed and started to stuff her belongings back into the bag.

"Isn't it bad enough I lost everything else? You had to take the only picture I have left now, too?"

"That's the only picture you have of your family?" He didn't know why he said it. It wasn't as though he had any photos littering *his* mantel. It had never bothered him before. He'd never really thought about it.

Her lip curled back in a sneer. He'd known her less than five hours and he'd already seen that face far too much. "You went through my bag, genius. Did you see any family albums in there? I didn't exactly have time to pack before I left New York. For all I know, most of my stuff was tossed out in the street after I left. This—" she gestured wildly at the torn photograph "—was all I had."

He felt no triumph that she'd admitted she was from New York. It only told him how much he'd rattled her without even trying. "Maybe your mother—or your brother—has more."

She stiffened. An implacable coldness rolled over her features, closing out the emotion that had flared in her eyes moments before. Her face was now a carefully controlled blank. He was already coming to recognize that was the expression she feigned when she was at her most emotional, when she was feeling something she refused to let anyone else see.

"They're dead."

The flatness of her voice didn't fool him in the least. "I'm sorry," he said. The words made him feel like an idiot. He wished he hadn't said them.

She didn't acknowledge them. Once her bag was repacked, all except some underwear, she zipped it up and tossed it on the floor. She pulled the underwear on under the shirt, then crawled onto the bed.

"I bet you want to shackle me to the headboard?"

Of course he did. He hadn't expected to feel guilty about it. "You're not going to fight me?"

"I just want to sleep."

Grabbing the pieces of the photograph in one hand, she threw the other arm up toward the headboard and turned her head away as he approached. As he moved to fasten the handcuffs—one to the post, the other to her wrist—he couldn't help but be aware of the torn photograph she clutched.

"I'm sorry," he said again.

"It doesn't matter," she said, not looking at him. It was a

lie. They both knew it *did* matter to her. But there seemed to be nothing else to say.

It only took a second to fasten the cuffs. As soon as it was done, she slid down onto the bed and curled into a half circle, her back to him.

He stood there like an idiot, feeling like he should say something else.

What came out was, "I want to cut out early. I'll wake you."

She said nothing.

Flipping off the lights, he climbed onto the other bed fully dressed and lay there, waiting. Exhaustion dragged at him, urging him to close his eyes. Just for a second. That was all it would take.

He fought the impulse and made his breathing deep and steady. He didn't trust her not to try anything as soon as she thought he was asleep.

A few minutes later a whisper of sound put his body on alert. He listened carefully. What the hell was she doing over there? He should have searched her to make sure she didn't have a needle or something to jimmy the lock on the cuffs. It wouldn't be easy, but he wouldn't put it past her to try.

The noise was soft and shaky, the sound muffled.

It hit him like a fist.

Allie Freeman was crying.

It took all his self-control to bite back the curse that rose to his lips. The curse would let her know he was aware of her tears, and he had a feeling she would resent that knowledge more than anything. She'd finally given in to the tears only because she thought he was asleep. He sure as hell wasn't going to take that away from her. It looked like he'd taken too much away from her already.

So he lay there, frozen, wishing to high heaven there was something he could do, knowing any gesture he made would only make things worse.

And he'd thought he was immune to a crying female.

He listened as her quiet sobs slowly gave way to soft murmurs. Finally all he heard coming from her bed was the shallow hitch of her breathing. She'd cried herself to sleep.

He waited a few moments more to be sure she was out, then threw his legs over the edge of the bed. Moving silently, he crept to the door and slipped out of the room.

He closed the door behind him and pulled out his cell phone. The parking lot was deserted. He wasn't worried about being overheard.

He expected to get Newcomb's machine—it couldn't be three-thirty in the morning yet in New York—but the detective picked up on the second ring.

"Ross?"

He felt a jolt of surprise. "How'd you know?"

"Can't think of anybody else who'd be calling me this early."

"What are you doing up? Don't tell me you were waiting for me to call."

"Nah. I was up, anyway. I'm not getting a lot of sleep these days. So what's going on? You find Taylor yet?"

"Yes."

"And?"

"And this is a lot more complicated than you led me to believe."

Silence. "Which means you don't have him."

"Which means I ran into a complication."

"What?"

"There's a woman involved."

Newcomb's heavy sigh echoed across the line. "Hell, I should have called that one. Nine times out of ten the complication's a woman."

"This woman had Taylor after her. I've seen where she was living, and she acts like somebody who's been on the run for a while. Taylor's been following a trail that led straight to her. I think she's the reason he skipped town. He came looking for her."

"Why? Who is she?"

"She's not talking, but I found an ID on her in the name of Allie Freeman. That ring any bells?"

There was a pronounced beat of silence, then, "She worked for Chastain's company."

Hearing his suspicions confirmed didn't give Ross any satisfaction. "I knew she had to be involved with him. Did anybody ever talk to her?"

"No," Newcomb said slowly. "She disappeared around the time of the Mulroney murder."

"Hell, she has to know something about what happened that night. That's why Taylor's after her and why he took the big risk of skipping town just before trial. He and Chastain can't want her to testify."

"She given you any indication of what she knows?"

"Not a thing. All she's given me is that she's no fan of Chastain's and she's scared to death I'll turn her over to the cops."

"What are you going to do with her?"

"I'm going to find out what she knows."

"You've got her in custody, then?"

Barely. "Yes."

"Where are you?"

"We stopped for the night at a motel along Interstate 80. I'm heading back in your direction."

"Good. She sounds like someone we'd like to talk to."

I'm sure she is, but you're going to have to wait your turn.

He wrapped up the call quickly and hung up, feeling ill at ease without really understanding why. Fighting a yawn, he dismissed the thought. It was too late and he was too tired to be thinking clearly.

And there was still one thing he had left to do tonight.

Chapter Five

She came awake with a start, the same way she always did, with her heart pounding in her chest, her senses instantly alert, her mind racing to recall where she was and who she was now.

Nobody, was the answer this time. No, that didn't make any sense.

Her thought processes were muddled from exhaustion. However much sleep she'd managed to get, it wasn't enough. It never was. She couldn't remember the last time she'd slept more than four hours at a time. The exhaustion was simply a constant she'd gotten used to.

She yawned, then tried to bring her hand to her face to rub her eyes. Pain shot up her arm.

That brought it all back. Ross. The handcuffs. Furious all over again, she glared at the gleaming metal and gave her arm a few angry jerks. The tantrum felt kind of good, but all it got her was more chafing on her already sore wrist.

Where was he? Pushing to a sitting position, she glared around the room. The bathroom door hung open, revealing another empty room. His bed was almost undisturbed, a faint indentation on the spread the only indication anyone had lain there.

If there was any justice in the world, he wouldn't have

gotten a wink of sleep. The idea almost made her laugh. The bastard had probably slept like a baby, which was more than he deserved after—

She gasped, her empty hand instantly closing around nothing. Gone. The picture was gone. Her heart in her throat, she grasped around the mattress for the pieces.

Then she saw it. She blinked, desperation replaced with confusion. It was sitting on the nightstand.

All in one piece.

Not understanding, she reached over and gently picked it up.

The two pieces had been taped together, carefully aligned so that the jagged edges lined up exactly. The clear tape showed and the photo wasn't exactly as good as new, but it was as close as it was going to get.

She sat there for a while, staring at the image, feeling strangely numb. *He'd* done this for her. He'd put the photograph back together. But why? That was what didn't compute. The man had dragged her across state lines, humiliated and harassed her with no indication he gave a damn about her feelings. And now this.

The door swung open, sending a slash of sunlight across the bed. She turned her head against the glare and quickly shoved the photograph out of sight. She couldn't have explained the protective instinct if she'd tried.

The brightness dimmed momentarily when he stepped through the door. He flipped the light switch on his way in, filling the room with a dull glow.

"You're up," he said, barely looking at her. "Good. We need to get on the road."

He was rumpled and unshaven, still dressed in the clothes he'd had on the night before. He must have slept in them; it made sense, since he hadn't brought a bag of his own in last night. There was a green duffel bag in his hand now, and in the other, a cup and a paper sack. The blessed smell of coffee wafted to her over the stale mustiness of the room.

Dropping the duffel on his bed, he crossed to her and held out the hand bearing the food. "Here. Eat."

She hesitated. "Where's yours?"

Dark amusement flickered in his eyes. "Ate it on the way. Don't worry. I didn't slip anything into the coffee."

"And the food?"

"Also clean. I make no promises for future meals."

She took the cup, careful not to let her fingers brush his. "I'll be sure to keep that in mind."

"Good. I'd like it if we could get out of here without a hassle. Give me some and I won't hesitate to slip you something."

She sipped the coffee. It was just cool enough to be drinkable. "I make no promises."

"I didn't think so."

She shifted and brushed against the photograph she'd placed beside her. The reminder of what he'd done made her go stiff.

She stared into her cup. *Thank you.* The words were there. She knew she should say them, wanted to say them. But they stuck in her throat.

And then the moment was gone.

He started to turn away.

She jerked against the cuffs, rattling the metal against the bed frame. "Aren't you going to unlock these? I need to use the bathroom."

"You'll have to wait your turn. I'm going to take a shower."

"What am I supposed to do? Hold it?"

"You finish that coffee fast enough, you can use the cup."

"Or I can throw it in your face. That'd empty the cup pretty quick."

"Try it and you'll be using nothing *but* cups all the way back to New York."

"Then I'll have plenty to throw in your face, won't I?"

Shaking his head, he grabbed his bag. "Be good, Allie. I'll be out in a second."

"At least no one's forcing you to undress in front of them."

He stopped halfway to the bathroom. Something in his posture sent a frisson of alarm through her. Her pulse leaped in response. He turned back, his eyes narrow and gleaming with some emotion she couldn't quite identify. Whatever it was, it made her nervous as hell.

He dropped the duffel bag.

"You're right," he said. Jabbing his heel with his toe, he kicked off one shoe, then the other. "That wasn't fair."

"What are you doing?" she said, her voice admirably even. She knew exactly what he was doing, as she watched him plant his heel on the opposite sock and drag his foot out of it.

"Getting undressed." He tugged his shirttail from the waistband of his jeans.

"I don't know what you're trying to prove."

"Not a thing. I'm just getting undressed for my shower." He pulled the T-shirt over his head in one quick, smooth motion and tossed it aside, then stood there, bare-chested, watching her. His mouth tilted up at one corner. "What's the matter, Allie? You sound nervous."

She tried not to look, she really did. Tried to meet his eyes and not drop her gaze anywhere near that expanse of bare flesh that hovered just out of her range of vision.

"Pretty stupid question coming from the man who has me handcuffed to a bed and is now taking his clothes off."

"We both know I'm not going to come near you. If I'd wanted to, I would have done it already."

She meant to roll her eyes. Really. Truly. But somehow she found herself staring at his chest instead.

A rush of pure feminine appreciation coursed through her. He had a body to match the chiseled hardness of his face, all rough-hewn muscle and firm flesh. Dark hair swirled around his flat nipples, then arrowed downward, over the ridges of his belly, and from there, even lower—

She jerked her gaze back up, already knowing before she saw his face that she'd looked just a little too long.

His expression, smug, sleepy-eyed masculine satisfaction, only confirmed it.

And then her attention drifted downward again, the second she heard him unfastening his belt.

She cleared her throat, once more jerking her gaze away. "So what's this supposed to accomplish?"

He tugged the belt loose from his pants, the length of leather snapping in the air as it broke free. "I thought it was what you wanted. Everything nice and even between us." He popped the button on his jeans. "Or were you spouting off again just to tick me off?"

The rasp of a zipper sliding down filled the air.

"Fine. If you really want to show me what little there is to see, I won't stop you."

He hooked his thumbs into the waistband of his jeans and slowly eased them down his thighs. "That would hurt a lot more if you weren't blushing like a little kid."

"Strip down in front of little kids that often, do you?"

He kicked off the jeans, leaving him in only a pair of all-too-brief boxer shorts. "Nope. Just loudmouth women who maybe aren't as tough as they like to pretend."

"Is looking at you supposed to be that tough? What's the matter, Ross? Got some gruesome scars?"

"See for yourself."

And with that, he shucked the boxers and stood naked before her.

She looked. Heck, she was only human. She'd never had a naked man just stand in front of her and dare her to look at him.

And part of her knew she couldn't look away if she tried.

There was nothing little about him. That was as annoying as it was fascinating. He was big and muscular all over, from the broad shoulders to the massive forearms to the powerful thighs and in between.

Nope. Nothing little there.

"There. We're even."

The satisfaction in his voice jolted her out of her fascinated stupor. She suddenly realized her mouth was hanging slightly open—and was dry as dust inside. She clamped it shut. Too late.

"Just like I thought. Not so tough."

If she'd had anything close at hand but the precious coffee, she would have thrown it at him. It took everything she had *not* to, anyway. He wasn't worth it. Instead, all she could do was sit there, seething as he picked up his bag and sauntered smugly into the bathroom.

Don't look at his butt. Don't you dare look at his butt.

She did.

It was just as tight and firm as the rest of him. She watched the muscles shift as he walked, unable to look away.

The worst part was knowing she would have kept on looking if he hadn't closed the door behind himself with a gentle snick she felt as keenly as a slam.

Well, she told herself, she wasn't dead yet, and the man had a mighty fine ass to go with the rest of him. *Appropriate enough since he* was *one,* she steamed. She couldn't feel too bad about looking.

It didn't make her feel any better. Of all the men for her to finally notice, why did it have to be him?

She was losing her mind. Because of him. Just another knock against him.

Disgusted with herself, she ran her gaze around the room. It was pulled to the pile of clothes he'd left where they fell.

Including the jeans where he'd kept the handcuff keys the night before.

No way. It couldn't be.

But it wasn't like he'd had anywhere to keep the key on him when he'd walked into the bathroom.

Triumph surged in her. She couldn't keep the grin off her face. "Oh, please, let that little show come back to bite him in the ass."

Don't think about his ass.

She shoved the image aside to focus on the bed frame. For once luck might be on her side. The frame was thin metal instead of a heavier wood. Locking her to it might not be as secure as he'd thought. At the very least it gave her some maneuverability.

She carefully placed the photograph on the nightstand between the two beds and jumped to her feet. Grabbing the mattress with her free hand, she started to nudge it off the bed. It wasn't easy. The thing was heavy and cumbersome. She almost fell on her butt more than once. But gradually, with one eye on the bathroom door and her ears peeled for every sound, she managed to shove the mattress off the frame and onto the floor.

The bed frame wasn't exactly weightless, but with both hands, one of them cuffed, gripping the metal, she was able to pull the bed across the carpet. It was slow going, and she had to make as little noise as possible. She cringed at every creak and groan of the frame. Every second she was keenly aware of the shower running. At any moment she expected him to burst out of the bathroom and stop her.

Finally she managed to get within body length of the pants. She couldn't have moved the bed more than a few feet. How long had it taken? Tension thrummed in her veins. There was no time to worry about it. Stretching as far as she could, she reached toward the jeans with one foot. If she could just hook her toe through the belt loop...

It still remained inches out of reach. She stretched farther, until it felt like her shackled arm might be torn from its socket.

Just when she was about to give up, she made contact and hooked her toe through the loop. She bit her lip to hold back a shout of triumph, and only allowed herself a silent cheer once she was sure she had the loop clamped between two toes.

With the key now within her grasp, the sense of urgency grew tenfold. Holding her breath, she pulled her leg back as fast as she dared. At last the jeans were firmly positioned within arm's reach. The air shuddered from her lungs as she grabbed the pants. The key was in the left side pocket.

Right next to the keys to his truck.

She felt almost giddy with success. Two seconds later all the keys were in the palm of her hand.

Thanks, chump.

There was no time to savor her triumph. She moved faster than ever. In the bathroom, the shower continued to run, the running water a steady hum through the pipes lining the walls. With one ear monitoring the sound, she unlocked the cuff binding her to the headboard. The wrist throbbed and the hand was asleep. She shook it to get the blood circulating again, but didn't waste time rubbing at the soreness before reaching for her clothes. There wasn't time. He could emerge at any moment.

She pulled a rolled-up pair of jeans out of her backpack and yanked them on. The button was barely fastened before she grabbed the photograph from the nightstand, hoisted the backpack over her shoulder and bolted for the door.

Flinging it open, she took two steps into the morning glare. The light was blinding. She turned toward the truck.

And stopped in her tracks.

A man stood beside the truck, peering in the window. He was tall and dangerous-looking, not the type of man she'd want to run into in a dark alley. Or even in a sunlit parking lot.

His appearance threw her, and she froze a split second too long.

Before she could convince her legs to cooperate, he turned and looked straight at her.

There was a subtle change in his posture, and she felt, rather than saw, the jolt of recognition in his eyes.

She looked left and right, gauging the possibilities of escape, not bothering to be subtle about it.

Like it mattered. He *knew*.

There was nowhere she could go. He'd catch her in either direction. She couldn't risk trying to outrun him. Reaching the motel office would only involve other people. That wasn't an option.

It was either him or Ross.

No contest.

When he reached into his jacket, her limbs sprang to life. Before he could withdraw a weapon, she spun around and ran back inside.

The door came with a dead bolt, a security chain and a lock on the knob. None of them was going to stop anyone who wanted into the room badly enough. She secured them all anyway, then glanced around the room, desperately seeking an escape. She could practically feel the floor vibrating as the man outside pounded closer.

There was only the front window next to the door. No other way out of this room.

That left the bathroom.

Damn it.

Racing across the room, she reached the bathroom door just as Ross was opening it.

She barely registered the shock that flashed across his face at her sudden appearance before shoving her way into the small room.

He grabbed her wrist. "How did you get out of those cuffs?"

He was already dressed. Thank God for small favors. They didn't have time for that. "We have to get out of here."

He dropped her wrist, apparently recognizing the no-nonsense tone of her voice. "Why? What's going on?"

She dodged around him and reached for the window. "A man in the parking lot. He was looking in your truck. He saw me. I'm sure he's coming this way—"

She didn't have time to finish the thought. They both froze at the sound of pounding on the motel-room door. Someone was trying to break it down.

"Is it Taylor?"

She froze, not sure how to respond. If she said it wasn't, would he want to go see who it was? Or would he even believe her? "I'm not sure," she hedged.

"Well, if it is, this'll save me the trouble of taking him later."

Before she could react, he reached into the duffel bag and pulled out a gun.

"Fine, you do that. But I'm getting out of here." She turned her attention back to the window. It had been painted over and wasn't budging.

Ross grabbed her arm. "Oh, no, you're not."

"You can worry about me, or you can worry about him. Your choice. But you can't focus on both of us, and I'm not going to stay here like a sitting duck when I'm pretty sure he's armed, too."

They both heard the outer door starting to crack under the force of the man's blows.

She felt Ross's acceptance before he responded. "Here. Let me."

Pushing the gun into the back of his waistband, he shoved her aside without a trace of gentleness, and slammed his elbow straight into the glass. It shattered, leaving a few large shards in the frame, which he jabbed out without missing a beat.

She hurled her backpack through the empty space, then went to boost herself through the window. He was already there, offering his cupped hands for her foot. Grabbing the sides of the pane, she slipped her foot into his hands and let him hoist her upward.

She fell facefirst, landing on her hands on the weed-choked gravel behind the motel. She didn't even notice the bits of gravel biting into her palms as she got to her feet and reached for her bag. She didn't have to wait for Ross. First his bag, then the man himself landed beside her. She didn't even want to know how he'd managed to fit through the window.

He was on his feet and had her forearm in an iron grip within a heartbeat. She didn't mind his touch this time. There were more important things to worry about.

The sound of the door to the room crashing open was a good reminder of exactly where they were.

"Come on."

They hurried around the side of the motel and peered around the edge to the front. The man wasn't in sight. The coast was clear.

She moved forward, ready to make a break for the truck.

Ross threw an arm up, holding her back.

"No."

She opened her mouth to argue when she caught his expression. She followed his gaze.

At least two of the truck's tires, the ones they could see, had been slashed.

"He covered his bases," Ross noted.

"Now what?"

"Now we steal a car."

She gasped before she had a chance to think about it.

He had the audacity to look down at her with what appeared to be amusement. "I told you, I'm not a cop. One of the perks of the job is that I'm not as bound by the rules as they are."

"And that includes stealing cars?"

"It does today. Especially if it keeps the owner from coming after us."

"What are you—" She followed his gaze to the car he was eyeing. New York plates. "That's *his* car?"

"Yep. Still feel bad about taking it?"

"No."

"Good. Let's go."

They ran to the sedan, found it unlocked and climbed in. It took Ross all of three seconds to hot-wire the engine. It sprang to life with a roar.

A quick glance in the rearview mirror revealed that their pursuer hadn't failed to notice his car had suddenly come alive. He was racing toward them. Not very fast, she thought. Maybe she *should* have tried outrunning him, after all.

Ross quickly shifted the car into gear and spun out of the parking lot in a plume of dust. The last thing she saw in the side mirror was a lone figure slowing to a halt, waving the dirt out of his face to catch a glimpse of his own car speeding away.

After a moment, she sagged back against the seat.

Her relief was short-lived.

After they'd gone about a mile, he pulled over. Then, as her eyes widened in shock, he clamped a handcuff around her wrist.

"What are you doing?"

"I always carry a spare pair." There was a plastic grip on the dashboard. He looped the other cuff through it and fastened it tight.

"But—" She lapsed into silence, the words failing to come.

"Speechless. I like you like that. What'd you think? That we're best buds now?"

Her jaw tightened. "Of course not."

"Right. I'm not letting you get away again."

"I'm sure that's what you thought the last two times."

"And you didn't get away then, either, did you?"

"Third time's a charm."

"We'll see. Look at it this way—now you can show me how you got out of those cuffs back in the room."

She sniffed and jerked away. "A girl's got to have some secrets."

He snorted. "Then you're doing pretty good for yourself, because last I checked you don't have anything but."

DOMINIC BRANCATO WATCHED as his vehicle rapidly vanished from view, disappearing into the sun. He let the fury curl through his veins until he could barely see through the haze of it.

The woman was proving to be more difficult than he'd expected. But then, he hadn't counted on the bounty hunter getting in the way. They were making him look like a fool who didn't know what he was doing.

He didn't like being made to look like a fool.

Putting his back to the road, Brancato saw the front-desk clerk peering around the corner of the motel at him curiously. That was just what he needed—for the kid to come over and start asking questions.

He turned on his heel and headed away from the motel as quickly as possible. The first order of business was getting away from here before the police arrived, as they no doubt would. The second was obtaining a fresh set of wheels.

He had a bigger problem than the car though. If he was lucky, Ross wouldn't manage to figure out how Brancato had caught up with them. It wasn't something he was counting on. Which meant that pipeline of information had probably just dried up. Things had just gotten more difficult.

Not too difficult, however. Ross had probably thought taking his car would keep Brancato from pursuing them. But he hadn't anticipated how helpful he was being. As soon as Brancato had a new vehicle, tracking down the old one would be a piece of cake.

That was what GPS was for.

Chapter Six

They rode in silence for more than an hour. Ross kept an eye in the rearview mirror for any sign they were being followed. He knew Allie was doing the same on her side.

They were probably both being paranoid. They'd left Taylor stranded. But he wouldn't put it past Taylor to do exactly what they'd done and steal a vehicle of his own.

Only when they had an hour's worth of road behind them did he let himself relax. A little.

"Allie?"

"Yes?"

A smug grin lifted the sides of his mouth. "So you admit that *is* your name."

She didn't turn from her window. "No."

"Then why'd you answer to it?"

"You were obviously talking to me. There's no one else in the car."

He shook his head. "You aren't going to give me an inch, are you?"

"Are you going to let me go?"

"No."

"Then you just answered your own question."

"Well, if you're not going to tell me otherwise, I'll stick with calling you Allie."

"Call me whatever you want. It won't make me her. Besides, I've been called worse."

"Haven't we all?"

She glanced at him askance. "In your case, I can just imagine."

"I'm sure you can. I'm finally starting to figure you out, Allie."

"Really?" she said, sounding amused. "And what brought on this flash of insight?"

"That little display back at the motel about stealing the car. It's pretty strange behavior for a criminal."

"I told you I'm not a criminal."

"The funny thing is, I'm starting to believe you. No matter how hard a time I have believing anyone involved with Chastain and Taylor is an innocent."

A grim smile touched her lips. "I didn't say I was that."

"Yeah, well, you haven't said a whole lot about anything. But I'm willing to believe you're not involved in anything illegal. Nobody who'd throw a fit over stealing a car could be much of a criminal."

"I did not throw a fit."

He ignored her. "Which leads me to believe you're not scared of the cops because you're wanted for something. You're afraid they'll take you back and make you testify."

"Nice try, Sherlock."

"Why else would Chastain want you dead?"

"I hope you're not deluded enough to expect an answer to that. You came up with the rest of that harebrained story on your own. Why stop now?"

"Look, no matter what kind of danger you think you're in, we can protect you."

She looked at him then, her face gone as stony and cold as her voice. "Can you really? Tell me, Ross. How did that man know where to find us? How, out of all the highways leading out of Chicago, did he track us down to that particular motel? Because we both know I didn't talk to anybody. But I bet you did, didn't you?"

He didn't want to think about Newcomb, didn't want to believe the man capable of it.

His silence was as affirming as any answer.

"Let me guess, it was someone with the police. Someone you trust, isn't it? Maybe even the person who sent you after Taylor. Someone who's somehow never managed to get the evidence to catch Chastain and had to watch him walk away every time? That's the person you trusted?"

Again, he said nothing.

She leaned closer, until she was practically whispering in his ear, the proverbial serpent tempting him into believing something he knew he shouldn't.

"So tell me again, Ross. Tell me how you can keep me safe from Chastain when you can't even keep me safe from the cops."

He recoiled from the idea so strongly she fell back in her seat. "Anyone who might have seen me with you could have figured out that the first thing I'd think of was try to get you back to New York. Taylor knows me. If he talked to any of your neighbors, anyone who might have seen me with you, he would have known exactly what I'd do with a witness."

A trace of pity entered her gaze. "Still believe all the cops are the good guys, do you? Must be nice. I had to face reality a long time ago. It's a rude awakening, let me tell you."

He smirked. "So now we're telling stories about ourselves, are we?"

She turned her back to him. "Forget it."

"No. Maybe I should tell you a little story of my own that should let you know exactly who the good guys and bad guys are in this little game you're playing. Then maybe you'll understand what kind of man it is you're protecting."

"The only person I'm protecting is myself."

"Chastain's a murderer, Allie. He's responsible for the deaths of more people than I can count, innocent people who didn't deserve to lose their lives because one lowlife son of a bitch wanted something he couldn't have."

She shrugged one shoulder. "Tell me something I don't know."

"And that means nothing to you? Are you really so selfish that you're going to let him get away with it?"

He waited for her reaction, expecting guilt, hoping he'd cracked her brave front just a little bit, at least enough to start wearing her down.

But when she looked at him, it was with eyes that were all too perceptive. "And who did he kill that you cared about?"

Damn. She was too quick. He returned his attention to the road. "What are you talking about?"

"This is personal for you. Why? Which one of those many people he killed mattered so much to you?"

An angry breath hissed out from between his teeth. "I promised you a story, didn't I? Well, here it is. It's about a bounty hunter named Jed Walsh. He was a good guy, the best. He did his job and he did it well. People respected him. He went out of his way to help people, and when he came across this kid living on the streets, he took him in."

"How old was the kid?" Her tone was so flat he couldn't tell if she was really interested or not.

"Thirteen. A real punk, too, the kind of kid most people would call the authorities about and be done with it. Lippy. Plenty of attitude."

"Some things never change," she murmured.

"And some things do. Jed took the kid under his wing, taught him the business, taught him about pride and responsibility, taught him what it was to be a man."

Ross swallowed over the lump in his throat. He hadn't thought the onslaught of memory would hit him like this. He could picture Jed's face when he first met him, the way he'd looked like the scariest mother he'd ever seen. Twenty-five years later, weathered with age, trapped in a body that didn't react the way it used to, he'd still been the strongest guy Ross had ever known.

"What happened to him?" Allie asked softly.

"He finally retired, long after he should have, only when his health wasn't so good and he finally had to admit it was time. He'd managed to buy the building he lived in with the money he'd saved over the years, thought it was a good investment. He had good instincts. A few years ago when the area started to undergo gentrification and all the developers started swooping in and buying everything, the property value skyrocketed. Jed was suddenly sitting on a prime piece of real estate. And your buddy Chastain came sniffing around, wanting to buy him out."

"He's not my buddy." There was a threat in her tone, a warning that she'd hurt him if he said it again.

He ignored her. "Jed wasn't interested in the money. The place was his *home*. He just wanted to live there in peace. And Chastain wouldn't let him. He decided he wasn't going to take no for an answer. He set your other pal, Taylor, on him. That's what Taylor does, you know. Convinces people to sell, makes things tough for owners." He shot her a look. Her face betrayed nothing. "Yeah, I'm sure you know everything about that. Little things started to happen. Windows being broken. Power and water being cut off over and over again. Tenants started moving out of the building and Jed couldn't replace them.

"But Jed was too damn stubborn. He'd spent his whole life dealing with lowlifes. He wasn't going to be scared out that easily.

"Then one day Taylor paid him a visit. Taylor walked out of the building. Jed didn't."

"He killed him?"

"Jed died of a heart attack. Funny thing, though. He had a heart condition. He had these pills he was supposed to take if he started having chest pains. They were right there on the table next to his chair the last time I saw him that morning. When the paramedics came that night, Jed was in the chair, dead. There were no pills anywhere in the apartment."

"And you think Taylor took them?"

"I know it. Jed had to pop those things every time he even *thought* about Chastain and Taylor. And then the man shows up at his apartment? The coroner said Jed died of a heart attack right around the time Taylor paid him a visit that afternoon. Not hard to connect the dots, is it? I know what happened, everybody does. That son of a bitch stood there and watched an old man die to get his hands on a piece of land. A man's life for prime New York real estate. Great deal, isn't it?"

"I'm guessing Chastain bought the building," she said.

"Yeah. One thing Jed wasn't so good about was making out a will, said it was bad luck to talk about that kind of stuff. He didn't have any legal heirs, so the property was put up for auction. Chastain picked it up for a song. It's a bunch of condos now. It took all of an hour to level everything Jed worked for all his life."

She was quiet for a moment. Then, "I'm sorry."

He could tell she meant it. But that wasn't worth a thing if she wasn't willing to do anything about it. "Yeah. So am I. That's the man you're protecting, Allie. And don't say you're not. If you know something and aren't coming forward, then you're helping that bastard. No matter what you say."

She studied him out of those solemn black eyes. "What would you be willing to do to see Chastain punished?"

His answer was swift and immediate. "Anything."

She turned her face away. "Believe it or not, so would I. But even if I could help you, you don't need me. You went through my bag. You know I read the papers. I know they have the murder on tape. They've got him."

"It's not a slam dunk. They could use an eyewitness to the argument Chastain and the Mulroney woman had before he killed her. It would help cement the motive."

She shook her head. "If I could come forward, I would."

"Then let me help you."

"You can't. No one can."

"Bull. I told you, I can protect you."

"And I told you. No, you can't."

There was no anger in her words, only resignation and a trace of regret.

Allie closed her eyes and curled up against the door, as if just talking about it had worn her out. And she hadn't said a damn thing.

He knew the story of Jed's death had gotten to her. He'd seen it in her face. She wasn't hardened against it. But whatever was holding her back was more powerful than anything he could say.

He needed to know what that was, even if it meant finding out everything there was to know about Allie Freeman.

The only real question was who he could trust to dig into her past.

It was too important to depend on someone he didn't completely trust. As much as he didn't want to believe it, that ruled out Newcomb. He was the only person who'd known what highway they were on. With that information he didn't even need to know which motel. Ross had given them enough time to search every motel along the highway until they found the right one.

Newcomb had lied to him. He knew that now. The man's

reaction on the phone when he'd mentioned her name—it was so obvious now.

He didn't allow himself to examine the sting of betrayal he felt that Newcomb might actually be working with Chastain, may have been all along. It did make a certain amount of sense, though. Chastain hadn't gotten by this long without having someone within the police force on his payroll. But the idea that it could be Newcomb…that hurt.

He pushed the thoughts away. There was no time for them. Newcomb could be dealt with later.

No, he couldn't trust Newcomb.

Which meant he had to find someone he could.

"DAMN IT. STOP CALLING already."

Taylor tossed his cell phone onto the passenger seat after checking the number of the incoming call. Chastain had been calling nonstop since last night. Taylor didn't have anything new to report and he really didn't want to explain how his car had broken down outside of Chicago and he'd spent half the night looking for a new one, finally getting back on the road a few hours ago.

Or how he might be on nothing more than a wild-goose chase.

His gut told him he wasn't. Not that Chastain was likely to put much stock in that.

His eyes dropped to the grid on the handheld device in front of him. The slowly moving dot represented the car he was following. Despite the hours he'd lost, the vehicle hadn't gotten as far as he'd feared. It had stopped for a while, and he'd actually thought he could catch up to it. Then it had started moving again.

No matter. He'd catch up soon enough.

It was only a matter of time.

Chapter Seven

She was blind.

She lurched forward in her seat, suddenly terrified. She couldn't see a thing. He'd done something to her. Everything was black.

No, not everything. Gradually the dim glow of the headlights floated out of the darkness. A distant light grew closer, until they passed under it, allowing her to see what it was. A light on the highway.

It was night again. She'd been asleep.

That was more confusing than the darkness.

She shook her head to clear the fog from her brain. It was impossible. She never fell asleep that easily, never came awake so smoothly. She was too on guard at all times for that.

It didn't make any sense.

"Morning, sunshine."

She felt Ross's eyes on her. She didn't look at him, didn't want him to see her confusion.

"Doesn't look like morning to me," she grumbled.

He shrugged. "Night and early morning don't look that different when the sun's not up yet."

Alarm shot through her. "Did I sleep all night?"

"No. The sun went down half an hour ago."

"Cute," she muttered. She couldn't have been asleep for

more than a couple of hours, then. She still felt strangely well rested.

She didn't want to think about why she had no trouble sleeping around this man when she hadn't had a solid night's rest in over a year. She usually slept in fits and jerks, unable to relax enough for more than brief periods of time to get any real sleep. Yet being around this guy was enough to knock her unconscious.

A suspicion crept into her thoughts. She eyed him across the seat. "You sure you didn't put something in that soda you gave me at lunch?"

He grunted. "Guess you're one of those people who's a bear when they first wake up, huh? Not that I've ever seen you act any other way, so maybe that's just your personality."

"Sorry. I'm just not used to sleeping this much." Especially when she was supposed to be plotting her escape. "Where are we, anyway?" No doubt closer to New York than they had been. A bright light outside grew nearer, then passed over them before being left behind. The lights on the highway were spaced far apart. She and Ross weren't on the interstate now, most likely a smaller highway, much like the ones Ross had kept them on all day in an attempt to lose anyone who might be following them.

"Somewhere in Pennsylvania."

"You sure?"

"I managed to pick up a map. It's amazing how much easier things go when you're unconscious."

The headlights swept over a sign in front of them, reminding her of a more pressing problem.

"There's a rest area. Pull in."

He made no move to ease off the accelerator. "I stopped half an hour ago for gas. You missed it."

"You could have woken me up."

"I like you better conked out."

"Why don't you just club me over the head and drag me by my hair?"

"Don't tempt me."

The turnoff to the rest area appeared up ahead, rapidly growing closer. "Pull in. I have to use the restroom."

"I'm not going to lose any more time on the road. You'll have to wait until I stop for gas again."

"You ever tried to stop a woman from heeding the call of nature, Ross? Because if I'm going to spring a leak, I promise, it's going to be more uncomfortable for you than it is for me."

He didn't react at first. Just when she was about to protest, he swung the wheel at the last possible moment, carrying them onto the off-ramp.

The rest stop was a short, squat building, probably no more than a restroom on either side and a common area with vending machines in the middle. A few semis and a couple of cars were parked in front. As he pulled up, a woman holding the hand of a little girl came out of the restroom on the right side of the building and started toward a small car. Ross parked on that side of the rest stop, as far away from the other vehicles as possible.

"We'll wait until they're gone," he said.

"I'm not going anywhere." *Yet.*

A man emerged from the center of the building with several snacks and joined the woman in the car. A few minutes later, they departed, one big happy family.

She jerked against the handcuffs. "Now can we go?"

Ross didn't move, surveying the building for so long she finally heaved a frustrated sigh. At last, he shoved his door open. Climbing out, he shoved his gun into the back of his jeans, pulled the shirttail over it to conceal it and rounded the car to her side.

Opening the door, he peered in at her. "This is how it's

going to work. We'll walk to the restroom side by side, perfectly normal. I'll knock when we get there. If no one responds, I'll stick my head in and make sure it's clear and there's not another exit. If anyone's in there, we hightail it back here immediately and wait until they're gone to try again. You have two minutes exactly before I come in after you. Got it?"

"Should we synchronize our watches?"

He reached for the handcuffs, the key in his hand. "You're not wearing one."

She grimaced as he unfastened the cuff from the dash, slipping the loose end around his right wrist in one quick motion. His eyes darted over the vicinity, examining every inch, every shadow.

Sliding out of the car, she reached for her bag.

"Leave it," he ordered.

"I need to freshen up."

"You mean you need to keep your bag on you so it'll be easier to make a break for it. Leave it."

She did her best to tamp down her anger, but knew he probably sensed it all the same. The man was too good at reading her. Not that it took any skill to know what she'd planned to do—and still did.

Rising to stand beside him, she quickly slammed the door shut and bolted toward the restroom, forcing him to move with her. "Let's get this over with."

She could feel him scanning the area as they walked. For her part, she kept her eyes on their destination, paying no attention to anything but getting to the restroom. She was going to have to act fast if this was going to work. "Aren't you worried people are going to wonder why you're walking to the women's restroom with me?"

"Maybe we're newlyweds who can't keep our hands off each other."

"So we stopped for a quickie in a rest-stop women's room? Ew."

"We *are* holding hands."

"No, we're not."

"That's not what it'll look like to anyone watching."

He was right, of course. In the dim beams of the parking-lot lights, all that would be visible to anyone on the other side were two shadows, arms moving together in perfect sync.

"You've thought of everything, haven't you?"

"Remember that."

The restroom was on the east side of the building on the edge of the developed part of the lot. Just beyond it, the same trees that surrounded the building on three sides formed an impenetrable wall.

When they made their way up the path, Ross stepped slightly forward. The better to check the facilities out before he let her in, she thought in annoyance.

He didn't get a chance. The door swung open before he reached it.

A woman in worn jeans and a flannel shirt, her dark curls tucked into a baseball cap, stepped out of the room. She drew up short and looked at them in surprise.

Quick thinking paid off again. When the moment went on a beat too long, Ross's prisoner stepped closer to him and grabbed his arm, hiding their linked wrists from view. She opened her eyes as wide as possible and blinked rapidly at the other woman.

"My, did you go in there all by yourself? I was so scared I had to have Billy Joe here come with me."

The trucker all but smirked. "I know how to handle myself."

Ross reached over and patted the hand she was sliding up and down his arm. "Maybe we could ask this nice lady to go in there with you and keep you company so you don't get afraid in there all by yourself."

She kept the guileless look on her face, but inside she froze. The last thing she needed was someone watching while she tried to make her escape.

She forced a laugh. "Don't be silly, Billy Joe. We don't wanna hold her up. It's gotta be fine. She made it out okay. That makes me feel so much better."

She gave the cuffs connecting their wrists a meaningful tug. *You really want to explain to the nice lady why you've got me in handcuffs?*

She sensed him getting the message, and his displeasure.

"I take it the coast is clear then?" he said amiably to the trucker.

The words served their purpose, keeping the woman's eyes on his face while his free hand subtly moved downward and unsnapped the cuffs with a barely audible click.

Neither of them moved, waiting to see if the other woman had noticed.

There was no sign that she had. "All clear. See for yourself."

With that, the trucker shoved the door open.

"Great. Thank you so much." Before Ross could respond, his now-freed prisoner bolted, slipping inside. As soon as she was through, the door swung shut again.

She heard the trucker tell Ross, "A lady needs her privacy." No doubt he'd started to follow. The words barely penetrated. She had already zeroed in on her target.

There was a window on the far wall. Perfect.

Practically flying, she crossed the room and threw the window open. Then she turned and scanned the facility for anything she could use as a weapon.

The only possibility was a round metal trash can about waist-tall. It would have to do. She pulled out the garbage bag inside and tested the can's weight. It was heavy enough to do some damage, but not so much that she couldn't lift it. Grabbing it in both hands, she ran back toward the door.

She was just behind it when the door was eased open an inch.

"Allie?"

Ross. She lifted the trash can and held her breath.

The gap widened further.

"Allie, answer me."

A gust of air blew in from the window.

He must have felt it. He shoved the door open all the way and stepped in.

She swung the can.

It glanced off his head with a jarring thud that jolted down her arms. He pitched forward, falling facedown on the floor. The back of his shirt flipped up, revealing the gun.

Heaving the can aside, she paused just long enough to grab the weapon. If he did manage to try to come after her, he'd find it a lot harder to take her if she had the gun.

She didn't stop to see if she'd drawn blood. She couldn't let herself feel guilty. He was going to get her killed if she didn't get away. He'd given her no choice.

She ignored the small bit of relief she felt when she heard him groan as she dashed out the door.

She moved quickly back toward the car, not running, but walking at a fast clip. She couldn't afford to draw attention to herself; couldn't afford to stroll, either. For all she knew, he'd be right behind her at any second.

Opening the passenger-side door, she reached inside. Her hand closed around her backpack and lifted it off the floor onto the seat, so she could climb inside without tripping over it.

A hand clamped down on her other arm, jerking her back. The gun tumbled from her fingers, clattering onto the floor.

Fury exploded in her veins.

No! He couldn't stop her. Not again.

She pulled on her arm and threw her head back, ready to scratch and claw and do whatever it took to get away.

Her eyes locked with those of the man behind her.

The breath jammed in her throat.

It wasn't Ross.

Roy Taylor loomed over her, his eyes as dead as she remembered. His grin was feral, lipless and toothy.

She never saw the hand coming toward her face before it struck her. Pain exploded behind her eyes. Her head whipped back. The taste of blood filled her mouth. She blinked to clear her suddenly dazed vision.

Then all she saw was him. He shoved his face into hers. His hot, ripe breath blew into her face, filling her lungs. She wanted to gag.

"That's just for starters. I owe you a lot more than that, and believe me, you're going to get it." He jerked on her arm. "Now come on. You're coming with me."

A LOUD GROAN FILLED Ross's ears. It took him a second to recognize that the noise was coming from him.

He blinked against the dull throb pressing at the back of his eyes and found himself staring at an ocean of gray. Concrete. The same concrete his face was resting against. The floor in the women's restroom.

"Damn it, Allie. You're going to pay for this one." He didn't care if her kidneys exploded. She wasn't going to see the inside of a restroom the rest of the way back to New York.

Ignoring the pain in his skull, he shoved himself to his feet and stumbled to the door. The room swam in front of him. He shook his head to clear it, then winced at the sharp pain that shot down his neck. He couldn't have been out for more than a few seconds. She couldn't have gotten far.

He took two steps out of the restroom. His irritation faded as he took in the scene in the parking lot.

A man had his hands on Allie, his back to Ross. It didn't matter. Ross would have recognized that bastard anywhere.

Taylor was trying to pull Allie with him. She wasn't having any of it, struggling all the way.

Ross started forward, Taylor's name on his lips, ready to draw the man's focus away from Allie. He reached for his weapon, only to realize it wasn't there. She must have taken it.

His attention on her, Ross absently registered another vehicle pulling into the parking lot.

Then Taylor backhanded Allie.

Her head snapped backward. Blood sprayed in an arc from her mouth.

Shock caused Ross to lose a step. Fury made him move faster.

Allie didn't give him the chance to help her. Taylor tried to pull her with him again, perhaps thinking she'd be docile now.

Obviously the bastard didn't know who he was dealing with.

Even before she faced forward again, she was lifting her elbow. Taylor might have seen it coming toward his face in the split second before she swung it at him. That didn't give him time to duck.

He definitely didn't see the knee she slammed into his crotch.

Howling in pain, he loosened his hold just long enough for her to shove him aside with the backpack she clutched in her hand, and move past him.

Ross drew to a stop, just as she altered direction and headed straight for him.

Her back to Taylor now, she didn't see what Ross did.

Taylor spun around, his face twisted with rage.

Except now there was a gun in his hand.

Ross lurched forward again.

Taylor raised the gun.

Ross opened his mouth to shout a warning, already knowing he'd never get it out in time.

The sound of gunfire drowned out the words.

For a split second, Ross's heart stopped.

But Allie kept rushing toward him. She never slowed, never missed a step.

Ross did. Shock caused him to stumble to a stop, unable to process what he was seeing.

A chorus of frightened and confused cries echoed from the other side of the lot. Ross couldn't make a sound. All he could do was stare at the bloody mess where the top of Roy Taylor's head used to be, just before Taylor's body crumpled to the ground.

It was like a bizarre dream where nothing made sense. Someone had shot Taylor. Blown off half his head.

Taylor was dead.

Stunned, Ross jerked his head to find the shooter. Then he saw the man climbing out of the vehicle that had just pulled into the lot. Gun in hand, the newcomer started to stride purposefully toward Ross.

Allie got to him first. She would have raced right past him if he hadn't reached out and caught her arm. When she struggled to get away, he dug in his heels.

She just pulled harder, flailing wildly. Reaching for her other arm, he forced her to face him. "Allie, it's okay. He got Taylor."

"I know that. I'm still moving, aren't I? I have to get out of here."

She wasn't making any sense. Maybe she didn't understand what he was saying. Heaven knew he was having enough trouble wrapping his head around it. "Allie, he shot Taylor. He's on your side."

She looked him straight in the eye. "No. He's not."

It wasn't the desperation in her voice or the words themselves that sank in. It was the look in her eyes—a look he'd seen before, the first time he'd seen her, back on that street in Chicago when she'd plowed into him and he'd grabbed her. She'd looked up at him with an expression on her face that he remembered in vivid detail. The utter panic in her eyes. The fear etched across every feature.

That was nothing compared to the expression she had on her face now.

Staring into that panicked look, Ross knew she wasn't exaggerating. For whatever reason, she was convinced the man meant her harm. And while Ross didn't understand how that could be, she was the expert. If she said they were in trouble, he had to believe her.

"Let's get out of here."

He could feel her relief in the moment before she took off, pulling him with her back into the darkness of the night.

Chapter Eight

It took less than five steps for Ross to take the lead. One moment she was pulling him toward the woods, the next he was disappearing into the trees, dragging her along with him.

She hadn't intended to go into the woods. She'd planned to go around the back of the building. Even with the cover of night, the sounds of them crashing through the undergrowth made their location obvious. Since it was autumn, a thick layer of fallen leaves coated the forest floor. The crunch beneath their shoes seemed to fill the air on all sides.

A gunshot echoed. She flinched. When she felt no pain, she kept moving. Not that she had a choice.

"Where are we going?" she hissed. Before the words left her mouth she heard another pair of footsteps crashing into the woods behind them.

He dodged to the left, then right, propelling them deeper and deeper into the forest with every step. She could barely keep up. It didn't matter. At the rate he was going, she doubted he'd stop if she fell. He'd just keep dragging her along.

"Faster," was all he said.

She struggled to keep pace. Every fallen branch, every root jutting out of the earth, was a trap threatening to ensnare her feet. After a while it seemed as though her feet were barely touching the ground, as though she were floating above it, her body propelled by his momentum.

Then, without warning, he slammed to a halt. She flew right into him. His arms immediately went around her, catching her almost in midair, holding her suspended above the ground in his arms. He must have spun around as soon as he stopped in order to catch her. Any doubt that he knew exactly what he was doing vanished.

She opened her mouth. "What—"

A palm slammed across her face. "Shh," he whispered, scarcely more than a whistle of air between his teeth.

She waited, listening.

It finally dawned on her that the sound of the other man's pursuit was coming from far away. With his speed, Ross had managed to put a great distance between them. She listened to their pursuer's progress. It was much slower, more awkward. He seemed to stumble about, cursing, tripping every other second.

Then, as if realizing they'd stopped, he did, too.

Ross slowly withdrew his hand from her mouth. Together they stood there, waiting.

She scarcely breathed, her air coming and going in silent, shallow gasps. The wind whistled past them, rustling what leaves remained on the trees. Pitch-blackness surrounded them. She could see nothing, feel nothing but the wind.

And Ross.

Was he really holding her up with one arm? She wasn't about to move her feet to test the theory, to see if they were touching the ground. All she knew was that it felt that way.

She felt his heart beat in his chest. The rhythm was slow, steady. She might be nervous, but his pulse told her he wasn't. She couldn't imagine his resting heart rate being any more even than this. Gradually, even as the knowledge there was someone out there waiting for them to betray themselves screamed though her mind, her pulse slowed until it was even with his.

She stood, safe in the circle of his arms. She had no doubt of that safety. Despite what his body told her, she knew he remained vigilant, in a silent standoff with whoever was out there, waiting to see which man blinked first.

It wasn't going to be Ross. He was so utterly still she got the impression he could remain that way all night. She realized that despite being held in position, she felt no urge to move, no restlessness.

It felt good. *He* felt good. Too good. But she'd known that. After all, this was exactly how it'd been when they first met. Had that only been a day ago? It didn't seem possible. This position was too familiar to her, his body too familiar, for a man she'd known for such a short time. As if his every muscle had been molded to fit with her body.

She couldn't help the shudder that rolled down every inch of her that was pressed against him.

He tightened his hold on her in response, as though afraid she was going to squirm for release, drawing her even closer to him.

An eternity passed.

Finally, softly, came the sound of the other man shifting from one foot to another, taking a step. She couldn't pinpoint his location, but it was nowhere close.

They waited.

The sound of a curse, low and guttural, told them he'd finally blinked first.

The four-letter word had never sounded so sweet as it echoed through the trees.

He began moving again. The crashing noise grew fainter. He was moving away.

Still Ross waited, until they didn't hear the noise anymore. He held her a few minutes longer. Only then, when it was clear the other man wasn't coming back, did he release her.

She rocked back on her heels, surprised to find she'd been on the tips of her toes the whole time.

Though she couldn't see him, she sensed Ross scanning the woods in every direction. "Now what?" She kept her voice at a whisper.

"We keep moving forward."

Of course they couldn't go back. Even if the other man didn't manage to find his way back there, and she didn't think he would, the rest area had to be swarming with cops by now. Ross wouldn't be any more eager to answer their questions than she was.

"Do you know where you're going?"

"Does it matter?"

No, she imagined it didn't. He'd known exactly how to get them to this point. She couldn't have done any better on her own, she admitted with some reluctance, if only to herself.

His hand clamped down on her arm again, unerringly locating it in the dark. She expected him to pull her forward.

He didn't move for a long moment, until she was about to ask him why. He spoke before she could.

"Are you all right?"

"I'm fine. A lot better than if those guys had caught up with—"

"Taylor hit you."

So he'd seen. Her cheeks still stung where Taylor had struck her. The copper taste of blood was just now beginning to fade.

It was nothing compared to what he would have done if he'd gotten her into that car.

"I'm all right," she said.

Ross still didn't move. She wondered what he was waiting for.

Then she felt his hand on her shoulder, sliding her backpack off. She started to protest, until she realized he was moving it onto his own. Finally, without a word, he started walking again.

She followed him. She didn't have to. The other man was gone. She could fight Ross. He didn't have his handcuffs anymore. She could escape. It might mean getting hopelessly lost in the woods, but she could get away from him, use his own tactics against him.

But she didn't. She let him lead her through the woods. She wanted to believe it was because she needed him to get her out of the forest. Or because she just wasn't up to arguing the point after everything that had just happened.

She couldn't even fool herself. Neither was the reason.

She trusted him. She didn't want to let go. Even when she knew she should.

So she followed him.

"YOU ALL RIGHT THERE, buddy? You're still looking a little ragged."

"I'm fine." Brancato forced a smile. No use ticking off the trucker before he dropped him off where he wanted. "Better now that you picked me up. You won't believe how many cars passed by without even slowing."

"I don't doubt it. Lot of people are paranoid these days, afraid they're going to pick up an ax murderer or something."

Brancato chuckled dutifully. If the man only knew.

"But when I saw you covered in mud like that, I figured, now that's a man who needs some help."

Brancato gritted his teeth. "You're right about that." He'd fallen more than once in the woods. The storm that passed through Illinois and Indiana must have made its way here. The area had been one big mud pit, and he'd fallen into every inch of it.

He saw the rest stop coming up ahead. Damn. The trucker had picked him up three miles back. He'd been walking in the wilderness for hours.

He gestured toward the sign. The mud had almost dried, making moving his arm hard. "You can just drop me off here. I'll get cleaned up and call a tow truck."

"No can do. There's big trouble there. Heard it over the scanner. Some kind of shoot-out. A man is dead."

Brancato smothered a grin of satisfaction. In the frustration of losing the woman, he'd almost forgotten about that. Killing Taylor hadn't been part of the plan, but damned if it hadn't been satisfying. It also made things easier, knowing he wouldn't have to worry about the other man interfering.

The trucker kept making conversation, probably happy for the company. Brancato tuned him out, silently seething. This was all Ross's fault. He didn't care anymore that killing Ross wasn't part of the job. He'd kill the bastard free of charge. After this miserable night, it was no more than he deserved, what they both deserved.

And he was going to give them exactly what they had coming to them.

THE MOTEL APPEARED out of nowhere, bright-colored lights sparkling through the trees. She could have fallen to her knees and wept with gratitude at the sight of it. They'd been walking for what seemed like hours.

"Stay here," Ross instructed, leaving her at the edge of the trees. "I'll get a room."

He approached the building without looking back, apparently trusting her not to try to run. Or else he knew she was so dead on her feet she could barely manage to stay upright. It didn't even occur to her to argue when he disappeared with her backpack.

Ross returned a few minutes later and motioned her out

of the woods. She took a tentative step, wary of the exposure. But the sight of him standing there, solid, immovable, was reassuring. She quickly crossed the distance between them.

"How'd it go? The clerk ask any questions?"

He placed a hand on her back and nudged her around to the rear of the motel. "Told him my car broke down a few miles down the highway. He didn't have any reason to believe otherwise."

She glanced uneasily at the highway as he unlocked the door of the room. A vehicle approached on the otherwise empty road. Her pulse kicked up a notch until it passed by without slowing.

"Are you sure it's safe to stay here? Shouldn't we keep moving?"

"The only way you're going to keep moving is if I carry you, and believe me, lady, my head hurts too much for that."

She shifted from one foot to the other, unable to avoid the small stab of guilt. "Sorry about that."

"No, you're not. But you will be."

She jerked her eyes to his face. His expression remained impassive. He shoved the door open and waved her ahead of him.

The room was nothing to speak of, standard-issue furniture just starting to look out of style. But it was warm and neat and reasonably clean. Heaven couldn't have looked any better.

"You're sure it's safe? They could check every motel along the highway."

He locked the door behind them and dropped her bag on the floor. "They could if we were on the same highway we were on before. We're back on the interstate. I figured they wouldn't be able to track us this far in the dark, and they'd probably stick to the road we were on, figuring we'd do the same."

"You knew where we were going? I thought we were just wandering."

"I memorized the map the last time I stopped for gas. It pays to know all your options. We're nine miles from where we started and headed in the opposite direction."

Nine miles! No wonder her feet felt like they were about to fall off. She reached for her backpack and, wincing at the weight, hitched it onto her shoulder. "Opposite direction, huh?"

"We'll be back on the right track in the morning."

That wasn't worth an answer. She might be yielding tonight; the morning would be a different story. She eyed the bathroom. "Do you want the shower first?"

His hand fell on her shoulder, halting her. "Are you going to tell me what that was back there?"

The answer was simple. "No."

He spun her around. "Not good enough."

For the first time since they'd left the rest area he let his anger show. She met it directly, too exhausted to work up any defiance. "It'll have to be. It's all you're getting."

"Don't you think I deserve to know why I'm going to die before they catch up with us?"

"Nobody forced you into this. You invited yourself along. Feel free to bail out at any time. You're lucky. You have the luxury of walking away."

"I thought I already made it clear. I don't. I'm just as involved in this as you are."

"That's funny. I doubt anyone would start chasing you if you went in the opposite direction from me."

"But I'm not going anywhere. That means they're shooting at me just as much as they're shooting at you."

"Then you've got no one to blame but yourself."

She tried to turn away again. He wouldn't let her. He grabbed her bag and threw it to the side, leaving her nothing to hide behind. She just stood there, feeling exposed.

"How can you be so cool? A man just got his head blown off back there."

"Less than twelve hours ago you were willing to throw me to the wolves to get that man. Don't pretend you care about him now."

"I had no problem dealing with Taylor. That was my fight. But someone else is involved in this, and I want to know who."

"No, you don't."

"Why don't you let me decide that?"

"Because words can't be unsaid. You can say that now, but you'll feel different if you actually know the whole story."

He took one menacing step forward, until he was staring down at her, their bodies only inches apart. She didn't retreat. She refused to back down, refused to let him intimidate her.

"Tell me who you are. Tell me who else is after you."

"Or what? Do you really think you can scare me, Ross? Everybody in the world seems to want me dead. What threat do you think you pose to me?"

"Just this."

He lunged forward before she could blink, grabbing her by both arms and pushing her back against the wall. He lifted her straight off her feet and pinned her there, almost at eye level. Her heart jumped in her chest as he held her gaze for a split second, his eyes dark with purpose. The corner of his mouth tilted in a ghost of a smile.

And then he kissed her.

At first she was too shocked to respond, to do anything but stand there, pinned to the wall by his body, as he slowly devoured her. His mouth was demanding, working against her own unresponsive one with practiced ease. Her lips fell open almost on their own, with the soft release of a sigh. His tongue plunged inside, stroking against her own in long, smooth thrusts that drove a moan from the back of her throat. It came out as he nipped her bottom lip, teasing it, taunting her. The sound echoed in her ears and rumbled through her body. And from a distance, she thought she heard him chuckle, low and so very self-satisfied.

She was beyond caring. Logic had fled, taking sense and reason with it. The taste of him was intoxicating, sending bubbles of pure sensation straight to her brain. She felt light-headed, unable to think, but more than able to feel. He was hot to the touch, all of him. Every inch of him was pressed against her, and every last bit of it was solid and hard. His muscular chest pressed against her breasts. She could feel his heart beating as madly and erratically as her own, a furious, clashing syncopated rhythm driving through them both.

His hands were no longer holding her arms. They didn't have to. He'd dropped them under her armpits, planting his palms against the wall. It wasn't his arms holding her up. It was the outthrust knee he'd driven between her legs. It was wedged right beneath her crotch, solid and immovable there against the apex of her thighs. She all but rode it, writhing against him as he seemed to be everywhere at once, driving her crazy. Taking her mouth. Lapping at the line of her jaw with his tongue. Nipping at her exposed neckline.

She threw her head back unconsciously to allow him greater access to the soft skin beneath her chin. Her hands caught in his hair and directed him upward. He obeyed, leaving a trail of kisses up her neck. She tilted her head to lead him back to her mouth. He dodged right, tracing the line of her ear with his tongue. His breath was warm against the moist trail he left there and she shuddered.

"Tell me who you are, Allie."

And just like that, the moment was over.

The flood of images, of memories, was instantaneous. It

all came back, everything. The heat of her reaction to his touch evaporated, replaced by cold fact.

You idiot.

She eased her hands out of his hair, barely able to restrain the tremor of revulsion, of recrimination, that threatened to rack her body.

How could you be so stupid?

She didn't want to touch him. She didn't even want to look at him. He was still pressed against her. It was all she could do not to shove him away and go running from the room.

How could you forget? How could you let him get so close?

It was Ross who pushed away, clearly reading the change in her. Try as she might, she couldn't keep her body from going stiff in his arms.

He surveyed her with cool detachment. Her gaze never wavered. Gathering all her strength, she threw her head back and smacked her lips. "Nice try, Ross. But you forgot, I don't scare that easily."

He only stared at her, his expression as unreadable as ever. He slowly ran his tongue over his bottom lip, as though savoring the taste of the moisture there. The taste of her.

It took every ounce of self-control she had left not to flinch, not to blink, not to react at all.

She put her palms against his chest and pushed him away. He released her, stepping back just enough to let her brush by. Inside she was shaking. She gave no outward sign as she snatched her bag from the bed and strode toward the bathroom.

He waited until she was almost there, just about to congratulate herself for her coolness.

"So why are you running away?"

She didn't miss a step, didn't say a word.

She let the slamming of the door behind her do the talking for her.

ROSS DIDN'T FOLLOW HER to the bathroom this time. He listened from where he stood as she locked the door and turned on the shower. He wasn't worried about her getting out of the room. He'd seen from the outside that all the bathrooms had bars on the windows. She wasn't going anywhere.

Besides, he couldn't have moved if he wanted to.

He exhaled slowly and waited for the stiffness of his body to ease. It was going to take a while. He could still feel her against him like an imprint on his skin. The smell of her hung in the air, or maybe he'd inhaled so much of her he couldn't shake it.

Damn. He slammed a fist against his forehead. What the hell was he doing? The woman could be a criminal. At the very least she was probably going to get him killed. And he wanted her as much as a teenager looking for his first time.

No. More. He'd never wanted it this bad, so much he could feel his skin crawl with the need to touch her, feel the nerves snap and tighten with the craving. If he went anywhere near that bathroom door, he'd break it down.

He knew it was a mistake, just as he knew he'd do it again if given half a chance.

Tell me who you are, Allie.

Damn. He didn't even know who she was.

She probably thought that kiss and everything that went with it was all an act. Well, it was better that way. Better than knowing the truth.

He wanted to know her secrets, and it had nothing to do with Chastain. He needed to know that he wasn't fooling himself trying to see something that wasn't there. He needed to know that someone in deep with Chastain and God knew who else hadn't managed to burrow so far under his skin he couldn't see straight.

He needed to get a grip.

With a growl of frustration, he forced himself to move.

Keeping an eye on the door, he reached for the phone on the desk. He'd tossed his cell back in Indiana. It would be too easy to trace them through it.

He'd given a lot of thought during the day to whom exactly he could trust. He wasn't feeling too confident about anybody at this point—if Newcomb could be turned, who was left?—but he had to take the chance. Nothing about this felt right.

Reggie Harris was not an easy man to get hold of. Next to nothing would drag him away from his computer. That was also what made him so good at his job. Ross listened to the phone ring five times on the private line few people knew about before going to voice mail, then hung up and dialed again.

Six tries later Reggie picked up. "What the hell do you want?"

Ross grinned. "I told you, Reg, if you want to get any business, you have to work on your people skills."

None of the irritation left the high-pitched voice. "Business is fine. You back in town or did they manage to hook up a phone in that cave you're living in?"

"Neither. I'm on a job."

"So much for retirement, huh? And now you're looking for information."

"I didn't call to hear the sound of your voice."

"Funny. What do you want?"

"You following the Chastain trial?"

"Not much to follow. Hasn't started yet. Don't tell me—you're looking for Taylor. I should've known."

"Here I thought you knew everything."

"Not everything, but what I don't know I can find out. Like now I know you're tracking Taylor. That could come in handy."

"I need you to keep that to yourself. Something funny's going on here. I've had enough people using my head for target practice in the last twenty-four hours to remind me why I got out of this game."

"Sounds like you're the one who needs to work on those people skills. Not that that's anything new. What do you need?"

"I need everything you can find out on a woman named Allie Freeman. Sound familiar?"

"Nope. Pretty plain-sounding name, though."

"She's connected to Chastain somehow. I need to know how. Also, I need everything you can get me on the case against Chastain. What went down that night, all the major players. I don't care how minor. I want it."

"Thanks. I *am* familiar with the concept of *everything,* you know. And how exactly am I supposed to get this to you?"

"I'll check back with you. How soon do you think you can get it?"

"How soon do you need it?"

"As soon as possible."

"I've got something else I have to wrap up first. Give me eighteen hours."

At this point, Ross was willing to take what he could get. "All right. Thanks, Reg."

"Save your thanks. Standard fees apply."

IN THE SHOWER, pellets of icy water beat down upon her. They couldn't wash away the feel of his hands on her body or the taste of his mouth on hers. They couldn't keep her from feeling the heat of him, every place on her body where he'd branded her with his touch. It was the coldest shower she'd ever taken, and she'd never felt more on fire.

She lifted an unsteady hand to her mouth, unable to stop shaking. Her lips felt strangely swollen. Her cheek burned from the rough stubble on his jaw. It was an odd sensation, one completely foreign to her. She'd never been kissed like that before, never been so thoroughly ravished by a man like that. There was none of the awkwardness of a first kiss, no clumsy fumbling or bumping of body parts.

Ross knew exactly what he was doing. There was nothing tender or tentative about the way he'd pressed her against that wall and completely dominated her senses with his every ministration. He knew the fierce emotion he was pulling out of her with each stroke of his tongue and nip of his teeth. He knew how to leave her filled with the taste of him, and leave her wanting more.

And she did want more, she thought, her heart sinking. She furiously rubbed at her raw mouth, trying to rid herself of the taste of his lips. It did no good.

It had been a scare tactic, she reminded herself with near desperation. That was all. He'd been trying to intimidate her, to frighten her into telling him what he wanted to know. And he'd failed miserably. Because fear was the last thing she'd felt.

She'd wanted everything he'd given her. No—she'd wanted more, and everything he'd pulled from her, every taste, every touch, every emotion, had been his to take. She would have given him so much more, until she had no more to give, if only he'd wanted them.

Tears pricked her eyes. That was what was so ridiculous. The kiss had been as calculated as they came, and he had her so mixed-up she couldn't tell. It hadn't been about passion or desire. He hadn't wanted her. He'd wanted what she wouldn't tell him.

And she'd wanted him just the same.

He'd been successful in one respect. Now she was scared. Scared of what he was capable of. Scared of what she now knew she wanted.

Scared she wouldn't be able to resist the next time. And there would be a next time. They both knew it.

And so she stood there, under the stinging spray of the shower, waiting to feel clean, waiting to feel free of him.

Waiting for a feeling she knew deep down would never come.

Chapter Nine

The sun rising over the city was one of the most magnificent sights in the world, especially with the view he had. Normally it filled Chastain with pleasure. On this particular morning, he barely saw it as he stared out the window, lost in thought.

The call had come at five in the morning from that lawyer he was paying too much for too little in return.

Taylor was dead.

He should have known something was wrong when Taylor hadn't answered his phone all day. Instead, he'd assumed Taylor had lost his phone. It seemed in character. He'd lost the woman more than once.

And she was still out there.

His attorney had said something about a man shooting Taylor. A man who'd last been seen in pursuit of a woman Taylor had been struggling with. And that was far more troubling than Taylor's death.

He swallowed hard. Someone else knew about the woman, might even have her at this very moment.

For the first time since this ordeal began, he felt the faint stirrings of fear in his belly.

The strange, sickening sensation was all it took to shake him out of his stupor. He recoiled from it, raged against it. Fear was an emotion for the weak, and Price Chastain had never been weak. He'd climbed his way out of the projects by doing anything he had to, and no one was going to send him back to any kind of hell as long as he had the will to stop it.

With fresh determination driving his movements, he stepped away from the window and retrieved his cell phone. It was better this way. Everything he'd ever managed to accomplish he'd done himself. He'd relied on others for too long. That was how he'd gotten in this mess to begin with. Well, no more.

Price Chastain could handle one stupid woman himself.

"I CAN'T BELIEVE you paid good money for this heap of junk."

Allie had to raise her voice to be heard over the engine and rattling frame of the ancient hatchback Ross had purchased first thing that morning. It ran well enough, but it certainly wasn't quiet about it.

"We needed transportation," he said simply.

"We could have taken the bus."

"Right. Because getting you around other people is a great idea. Besides, you really want to put a busload of people in danger? The way you were talking last night, I thought you didn't want innocent people to get hurt. Or was that just concern for me?"

"I've changed my mind. I would be more than happy to see you take a bullet."

"For you?"

"Or otherwise."

He gave his head a rueful shake and tried not to respect her bravado. It wasn't working.

There weren't too many cars on the highway at this hour of the morning. It wouldn't take them long to get to New York. He didn't intend to spend the time in silence, not when he could put the time to good use.

"I still want to know who else is after you."

"You can keep asking the same questions, Ross. It's not going to get you an answer."

"You'll have to answer eventually."

"Really? What are you going to do? Try to kiss the answers out of me?"

As soon as she said them, he could tell she regretted the words. She clamped her mouth shut, her lips forming a thin, angry line, and pointedly looked away.

He wasn't about to let her get off that easily. "Let's get one thing straight. What happened last night had nothing to do with this, and I think you know it. I don't operate that way. It happened because I wanted it to, and it was only a matter of time, anyway. I think we both know that. So don't be playing the victim and trying to hide behind hurt feelings to make yourself feel better about not telling me a damned thing. That's all on you. You want to be mad at someone, be mad at yourself."

She swallowed hard and smiled bitterly. "You're right, Ross. I *am* mad at myself, for a lot of things. It's too late to change any of that now, no matter how many questions you throw at me."

The anger immediately went out of him. He shook his head, barely able to control his frustration. "Damn it, Allie. When are you going to let me help you?"

A trace of sadness touched her eyes. "When are you going to stop trying to save me?"

He couldn't have explained the feeling that squeezed his chest when she said that. A knot formed in his throat from the way she looked over at him. He knew that look, bitterness tinged with defeat. He used to see it in his reflection every day. Sometimes he still did.

He managed to find his voice. "I'm not sure I can."

Allie turned away from him once more. He barely heard her answer.

"You have to. There's nothing here left to save."

He stared at her profile. Sitting there, gazing off at nothing, she seemed oddly vulnerable. In spite of everything she'd said and done, he'd never seen her that way. She was too much of a fighter. But looking at her now…

It took everything he had not to pull the car over, grab her by the shoulders and demand she tell him everything. He knew better than to pretend his interest was motivated solely by Chastain anymore. It had gone far past that. He might not know anything about her, but he cared what happened to her. After the number of close calls she'd had the past couple of days, it seemed clear that the danger stalking her was closing in. She couldn't outrun it forever, and the knowledge that he might not be able to protect her from it filled him with an inexplicable fear that was entirely too personal.

Not that he could say any of that to her. Doing so would require explaining things he wasn't sure he could, even to himself.

He kept driving. "So how old are you, anyway?" he said roughly.

Out of the corner of his eye, he saw Allie slowly turn her head to look at him. "I know you're a big, dumb jerk, Ross, but even you know better than to ask a woman that."

He shrugged. "I figure if you won't tell me anything a normal person would, I might get somewhere with a question a normal person wouldn't."

She leaned back against the door and regarded him. "Okay, I'll bite. How old do you think I am?"

He made a guess, then dropped a few years from the number to be safe. No woman liked to be told she was older than she was. "Thirty-three."

She laughed, the sound cold and humorless. "Try twenty-eight."

He couldn't help the quick glance he shot in her direction.

Her lips curved wryly. "I'm guessing you took a few years off what you really thought. Nice to know I look ten years older than I am."

"It's not that." It was true. It wasn't that she looked old. Her face could have been that of someone in her early twenties to her late thirties. He'd made his guess based on her eyes. The hardness there belonged to a much older woman, one jaded and weathered from all she'd seen. He would expect to see it in someone who'd lived a lot. Women of twenty-eight weren't supposed to have eyes like hers.

Hell. She was too damn young for him, too.

Not that that mattered, of course.

She shrugged a shoulder and faced forward again. "Running around avoiding getting shot at tends to add a few years to a person."

"And you were already one of those kids who grew up too fast."

She tipped her head in silent question.

"The picture in your wallet," he explained.

She knew what he was doing—trying to get her to let her guard down and tell him what he wanted to know by revealing seemingly innocuous details. She wasn't fooled. She also knew there was no danger of that. And it wasn't as though he could have read about any of it in the newspapers.

"Yeah, well, my mother wasn't a well woman. I had to help her, and after she died, I was working three jobs to raise my brother."

"Must have been tough."

She shifted uncomfortably on the seat. "What is this, true confessions time?"

"Just making conversation. How old were you when your mother died?"

"Eighteen. Jimmy was eight. She had a heart attack while she was on her hands and knees scrubbing some stockbroker's kitchen floor. There was no one to help her. She'd been dead for hours by the time anyone found her."

Even now, years later, she couldn't keep the bitterness out of her voice. Though she hadn't seen it, the image of her mother, lying dead on someone's floor, all alone, remained with her.

As soon as the words left her mouth, she wondered why she'd said them. She'd never discussed her mother's death with anyone, not even Jimmy.

Maybe it felt good to tell someone. Ross was the first person who'd ever asked, and though she knew he didn't genuinely care, that didn't change how nice it felt to talk to someone about it. About anything, really.

She'd spent a lot of time thinking about her mother in the last year, thinking about how hard Maura had worked for her children. As a child, she'd never understood how hard it was for her mother to be left with two children by two different fathers and no help. Then her mother had died and it was her job to take care of Jimmy. And she'd understood all too well. She would have done anything to keep food on his plate when she was hungry and keep him safe from harm.

She'd made a promise to her mother that she would take care of Jimmy if anything happened to her.

And she'd failed.

The thought reminded her of her mission, of what she had to do, why she had to escape Ross. No amount of conversation could change that.

"And your brother?" Ross asked, surprising her. She might have expected him to offer some empty words of sympathy at her loss, like most people did. Instead, he'd allowed her that brief moment of silence before asking anything else, leaving her to her thoughts, as if he'd understood how they'd naturally go to her mother.

He was a good man. She was coming to see that more

clearly now. He would be an easy man to depend on, to trust, and that was exactly what she couldn't do. Because good man or not, he was her enemy. He had to be. She had to remember that. If nothing else, his question offered a reminder.

"I told you," she said. "He's dead."

"He must have been young."

So young, she thought with a twinge. He'd had his whole life ahead of him. "He was seventeen, and so damn smart. He would have started college last fall."

"You must have been proud of him."

"Yeah. I was." Seeing the man Jimmy had been on the cusp of becoming had made all the sacrifices worthwhile. Then, in an instant, he was gone.

"What about your father?"

"He left when I was two. I don't remember him. Jimmy never knew his, either." She hesitated before admitting, "My mother never told me who he was."

"Ah."

"What can I say? My mother spent her life making poor choices." Just like her daughter.

"What happened to your brother?"

She tensed, knowing she shouldn't answer. But she couldn't help herself. It made the bile rise in her throat and the fury simmer in her gut. After all this time, the raw pain, the injustice of it, hadn't faded in the slightest. Because there'd been no closure, no justice. Not yet, anyway. But soon.

"He was murdered."

Again, Ross lapsed into one of those knowing silences. She went still, wondering what he was thinking. Had she said too much?

He cleared his throat. The voice that emerged was rough. "Why do I have the feeling Chastain was involved?"

"Because you think Chastain is involved in everything."

"So what happened?"

"I told you. He was murdered."

"How?"

She couldn't stop the words. They sprang forth, fueled by anger and pain. "He was shot in the head. They dumped his body in an alley like yesterday's garbage."

"Why?"

Because of me. "The police said it was a mugging." She knew better. There just hadn't been anything she could do about it.

"Did they ever catch who did it?" he asked gently.

"No."

There was no clue to his thoughts in his expression, as inscrutable as ever. "So then you know what it's like to have a killer go unpunished. And yet you still won't come clean about Chastain, even if it could mean the difference between him going to jail and going free."

"He's already going to jail. And I told you. I can't help you."

"I wonder what your brother would think about that," he said quietly.

An angry retort lay on the tip of her tongue. But her gaze went beyond him, to the window at his side. The words died on her lips.

A car had pulled up beside them, unnoticed in the heat of their conversation. Sunlight glinted off its windows, all except the open one on the passenger side. She could barely see the driver through the glare, but she could see what was in his hand.

A gun, aimed directly at them.

She grabbed for his arm. "Ross!"

He jerked his head to see the driver gesturing with his gun for them to pull over.

Ross slammed on the accelerator, instead.

The roar of the engine was pierced by the sound of the back window on Ross's side shattering into a million pieces.

She ducked, pure reflex. She practically heard the bullet whiz by her head as she did.

Another gunshot echoed through the car. She heard Ross's muffled cry just as the car swerved to the side.

"Take the wheel," he ordered, his voice strained.

She pulled her head up. Her breath caught in her throat. His left shoulder was drenched in blood, the stain on his shirt growing larger by the second.

"Take the goddamn wheel, Allie!"

The tone of his voice got a reaction. She reached across him and grabbed the steering wheel in both hands. She barely had a grip on it when he slammed his foot down on the accelerator again. The hatchback lunged forward. Beside them the other vehicle started to do the same.

"Cut him off. Now!"

She jerked the wheel to the left. The little car barely managed to make it in front of the sedan. It still clipped the bumper. Both vehicles fishtailed in opposite directions. She pulled the wheel hard to compensate, fighting to keep the car from going into a spin. The force of it rattled her arms all the way up to her shoulders. She clenched her jaw against the pain and held on tight.

She'd barely managed to get the hatchback moving forward again when they were rammed from behind. She was flung forward. Ross threw out his right arm, catching her before she flew into the dashboard.

"Right. Now!"

Instinct took over, obeying the order without processing it. They shot into an opening between a semi and a minivan. The blast of an angry horn burst from the latter. She ignored it.

The sedan was coming up on their left in the space they'd just vacated.

"Right. Now!"

She yanked the wheel again, finally clued in to what he wanted. The highway was dotted with traffic. They were approaching Philadelphia. The closer they came to the city, the more congested the road would be. Soon they'd be trapped in the throng of vehicles. They had to escape now.

The hatchback bounced onto the emergency lane, spitting gravel. Behind her, she heard the squeal of tires as the sedan followed.

Ross floored it. The little car was going as fast as it could, the frame rattling more than ever. It wasn't good enough. The sedan gained on them, its engine growing louder behind them.

She eyed the gaps in the traffic to their left. "Don't you want me to get over?"

"No. You've got an open road. Take it."

She complied, holding the wheel steady. Her grip on it was the only thing keeping her hands from shaking. They passed more cars as the traffic on the highway slowed. Still, Ross said nothing.

She couldn't see the other car behind them, couldn't see in the rearview mirror. But she could feel it growing closer.

The road curved. A blockade loomed up in the distance, cutting off the ramp the emergency lane turned into.

"The ramp is closed."

"Wait."

She watched with increasing trepidation as the roadblock drew closer and closer. The sedan's engine grew louder, cutting off the sound of the air whizzing by as they passed more-stationary traffic on the left. He wasn't giving up, either.

Why didn't he turn off? Couldn't he see the sign up ahead? Or was he so fixated on them they were the only thing he saw?

The roadblock loomed larger, its orange reflectors almost invisible in the bright sunshine.

"Wait for it…"

Thirty feet.

Twenty.

Ten.

The sedan gunned its engine.

"Now!"

She jerked the wheel to the left just inches before they struck the roadblock. Behind them came the sound of squealing tires and blasting horns as the car they'd just cut off slammed on its brakes to avoid them. A heavy explosion of crunching metal erupted behind them, the screech of steel and glass colliding over and over. She couldn't bring herself to look, couldn't do anything but hold the wheel in a death grip and stare straight ahead.

Then she heard another crash. To the right.

The sedan hadn't turned off in time.

She'd known it wouldn't be able to, but the noise was a comforting confirmation of the inevitable. She managed to draw in her first deep breath in several minutes. It still wasn't steady.

Ross slowly eased off the pedal. The hatchback's engine hiccupped ominously, grinding in discomfort. She experienced an uneasy moment. Then it adjusted to the new speed and kept on going.

"What'd I tell you? Good engine."

The words were cavalier, but they came out in a hiss from between gritted teeth. For the first time, she looked at him, really looked at him. The view wasn't reassuring. Sweat dotted his brow. His entire face was clenched with pain. The dark red smear now engulfed the entire upper left-hand side of his shirt.

She forced herself to keep her eyes on the road. "You need to go to a hospital."

"We can't do that."

"You've been shot!"

"It's just a graze. Barely scratched the surface."

"Your blood's all over the seat!"

"I'm fine, damn it." But the last words came out in a groan. She spotted the next exit up ahead. "That's it—"

"No." The order was typically sharp. He cast a bleary eye out the side window. "Where are we, anyway?"

"About a half an hour outside Philadelphia, I think."

He swore again, but this time the sound was resigned. "This must be someone up there's idea of giving me a sign."

Now he wasn't making any sense. "Are you delirious?"

"I wish. Keep driving. I know someone in Philly who can help."

"Who?"

"A doctor. Nobody knows about him. We'll be safe there."

"If you're still alive by the time we get there."

"I appreciate the concern. At least I know you're not going to bail on me and take off when I can't chase you down."

The thought hadn't even occurred to her. That probably said how far gone she was. But even if she was still desperate to escape him, she could never have left him like this.

Sliding over farther, she kicked his leg off the accelerator and stomped on the pedal. He didn't object, didn't make a sound other than a soft sigh that sounded almost like relief. She checked his face in the rearview mirror. He was struggling to keep his eyes open, the lashes fluttering erratically.

"Don't you dare pass out on me."

That got her a grin. "At least you'll have an excuse to slap me."

"As if I need one," she grumbled, but even she could hear the fear in her voice.

Doing her best to hold it back, she pressed the accelerator to the floor and pushed them onward.

Chapter Ten

Brancato regained consciousness slowly, drifting out of a dull haze into a world of pain. Then he couldn't move fast enough. He barely made it out of the wreckage and away from the car before the cops and paramedics descended.

He stood up on the incline overlooking the scene and briefly watched their efforts to check for survivors. As soon as they realized the driver was gone they'd start to canvass the area. He had to move.

He made his way back to the expressway, ignoring the pain he felt with every step. Once he got far enough from the scene, he might try to hitch a ride. Otherwise, it wasn't that far into the city. He could walk.

So close. It had been easier to find them than he, and most likely, Ross, had expected. Once the trucker had dropped him off at another rest stop the night before, he'd sat down with a map and a phone book and spent most of the night calling every business along the woods where he'd lost them in case they'd stopped. Ross had probably thought they'd gotten far enough away from the rest stop to prevent anyone from catching up with them. Sure enough, it had taken Brancato a while to make his way down the list to the motel where he'd tracked them down. From there, he'd watched them buy a car at a nearby dealership and had tailed them closely ever since.

If only he hadn't gotten impatient. He hadn't wanted to risk losing them in the thickening traffic and thought he could force Ross to pull over. So much for that idea.

It didn't bother him that they'd managed to get away. He savored the knowledge that he'd managed to get in one clean shot and drawn blood. Hell, for driving with one hand and aiming with the other, he deserved some kind of prize. The bullet should have taken Ross's arm off. The doctors still might have to cut the damn thing off. The thought was so sweet he had to smile.

Ross was seriously injured. That meant he had to seek out medical help. All Brancato had to do was check the hospitals to find him.

He was getting closer every time.

They weren't going to get away again.

DR. JOSHUA BENNETT was nothing like she expected. She'd imagined someone like Ross, tall and dark. Dr. Bennett was indeed tall, but no one would ever describe him as being dark. He was also younger than she'd imagined. A big, muscular man in his early thirties, he had a shock of blond hair and an open, easy smile that faded once he opened his door and saw them standing on his doorstep.

If he was surprised to see them, he didn't show it. He took one look at the two of them, Ross with his uninjured arm slung around her for the small amount of·support he'd allowed her to give him, and pulled them in without question.

"The kitchen's two doors down on the left. Get him in a chair."

"I can get myself in a damn chair," Ross grumbled.

Josh closed the door behind them. "She's the one who looks like she's in pain."

"Told her I didn't need her help."

"No, I mean the pain of having to listen to you moan and

groan." The doctor sent her an understanding smile that drew one of her own. "I'm Josh, by the way."

"Nice to meet you."

He shot a glance at Ross's grimacing face. "Now, if your feet work so well, you mind getting into the kitchen, instead of bleeding all over my house?"

Muttering under his breath, Ross started to shuffle in the direction the doctor had indicated. Josh disappeared into the other side of the house.

"He's right, you know," she told Ross as they moved down the hall. "You've been even crankier than usual. You always this bad when you're injured, or is this for my benefit?"

He glowered at her. "Why are you even here? I'd've thought you'd make a break for it by now."

"That's gratitude for you," she said, pulling out a chair at the kitchen table for him. She ignored the suspicious narrowing of his eyes and moved away. "You're right. I should have dumped your sorry butt on the doorstep and kept driving to Mexico. Or better yet, I should have shoved you out of the moving car, then backed up and run you over a few times. It couldn't have hurt your attitude any."

"Enough," he grumbled. "I got it already." He dropped into the chair. "What do you want, a medal?"

The doctor's reappearance cut off her reply. He had a medical bag in one hand and a bottle of tequila in the other. He set the bottle down on the table in front of Ross and spread the bag's contents out beside it.

Ross waved the bottle away. "I don't need that."

"You will when I start digging around in your shoulder for that bullet."

"It's not deep, it just hurts like hell," Ross groused.

"I think I can make my own diagnosis, thanks." Josh picked up a pair of scissors. "Sit up."

As soon as Ross obeyed, Josh started to cut off his shirt

with quick, efficient movements. She fought a wave of queasiness as he peeled the bloodied sleeve away from the wound. Ross winced at the tearing sound of the cloth detaching itself from the skin but said nothing.

No one spoke as the doctor bent over Ross's shoulder and probed the wound. She had to look away when he started digging for the bullet.

"You're right," Josh mused. "Didn't even hit the bone."

"Not my first time."

"That's not exactly a surprise, is it…" He tilted his head in her direction without taking his eyes off Ross's wound. "I'm sorry, I didn't catch your name."

Her eyes met Ross's. He shook his head. "Allie," he said as though daring her to disagree. "Her name is Allie."

She pursed her lips and said nothing. It didn't seem like the time to argue the point.

"Allie, then." If Josh noticed the sudden tension between them, he didn't comment on it. "You know I'd really prefer to be doing this in a hospital."

"We're not going anywhere near a hospital because we both know you'd have to report a gunshot wound to the police. Stitch me up and we'll be on our way."

"Can't stand to stick around for more than an hour, can you, Gid?" The doctor's tone was studiously light, but she caught the bite in his words.

A flash of something that looked suspiciously like guilt crossed Ross's face before his expression hardened again. "That's not it. You don't want to get mixed up in this situation, trust me."

"I don't know about that. If it wasn't for this, who knows the next time I would've seen you? Another couple of years?"

Ross coughed in discomfort. "Yeah, well, you know me. Not too good at keeping in touch. I don't even have a phone."

"Don't worry about it. I don't mean to bust your chops, but it would be nice to get a reminder that you're still alive every once in a while. I was under the impression you were tucked away nice and safe in that cabin of yours, and then you turn up here like this. It would've been nice to know you'd come out of retirement."

Unable to believe what she was hearing, she turned back around. She wasn't surprised to see Ross looking at her, waiting for her reaction, his expression resigned. "I haven't."

"You sure took quite a bullet for a man who's retired," Josh noted.

Ross looked like he'd give anything for the doctor to stop talking. "This isn't business," he said through clenched teeth. "This is personal."

Shock holding her frozen, it took her a moment to find the words. "You're not a bounty hunter?"

He didn't so much as blink. "Not officially. Not anymore."

"Then why—"

He cut her off with a glance in the doctor's direction. He clearly didn't want Josh to know more than he already did. "Like I said. Personal."

"So you lied to me."

"Call a cop."

She couldn't say anything, couldn't move. Couldn't do anything but stand there, staring at him with raw, impotent rage.

Then she spun on her heel and stalked out of the room.

A tense silence fell in her wake. The only sound was the soft snip of the doctor's scissors against the thread he'd just looped through Ross's flesh. Ross made no move to go after her, wouldn't have even if he could. She wasn't going anywhere. He'd ticked her off too much. She wasn't going to leave without having her say.

"I'm sorry," Josh murmured. "She wasn't in handcuffs or anything, so I figured—"

"Yeah, well, she has a funny way of slipping out of them."

"She wasn't acting like somebody who was trying to get away from you. I figured she was your girlfriend or something."

Ross couldn't even laugh at that, it was so ludicrous. "No way."

"Sorry. It just seemed like she cared about you, the way she was hovering."

Ross didn't know what to say to that. Why *hadn't* she run when she had the chance? It didn't make sense, at least not in a way that sat well with him.

Finished, Josh snipped off the last stitch and got to his feet. "All done."

"Finally," Ross grumbled. He started to rise, too.

Josh stepped in front of him, forcing him to fall back in the chair. "Now you can do something for me."

Ross frowned, instantly wary. "What's that?"

"Stay the night."

Ross immediately shook his head. "We can't do that."

"You two look like you've just come from running consecutive marathons. I've seen insomniacs who look better rested than you. Stay the night."

"If anyone finds us here—"

"That's not going to happen, is it? You wouldn't have stopped here if you thought anyone would connect us."

Ross didn't say anything.

Josh nodded, taking Ross's silence for the confirmation it was. "Don't worry, Gid. I'll be at the hospital all night and won't be back before noon. You have plenty of time to catch some shut-eye and get moving before I get back."

"Josh—"

The doctor wasn't listening to him. He grabbed his keys and the jacket slung over a kitchen chair. He called back over his shoulder on his way to the door, "The fridge is stocked.

Take what you need, clothes if you need them. Sorry about the mess. Don't worry about cleaning up after yourselves. It can't get any worse."

Josh paused at the door, his hand on the knob. A cloud passed over those sunny features. "I'll catch you later, Gid."

Ross could only bring himself to nod. And then Josh was gone.

Ignoring the sudden heaviness in his chest, Ross pushed to his feet and padded out of the room in search of Allie.

He found her in the living room, facing a wall of pictures. There were family portraits and photos of friends covering the whole damn thing, with more on the other walls. Josh with college buddies. Josh with colleagues from the hospital. Josh with cousins and aunts and uncles and two smiling parents. Josh was that kind of guy, a million loved ones who all loved him back. Allie's expression was blank as she went from picture to picture. He knew that look, knew exactly what she was feeling. He'd been there himself. Envy. Sadness. He didn't know what it was, but it was strong, a certain ache deep inside that was too complicated for a simple name.

He leaned against the door frame with his good shoulder and shoved his hands into his pockets. He kept his eyes off the pictures. "I thought you'd be halfway to Mexico by now."

She didn't look at him. "Would you blame me?"

"You bet I would. I got shot because of you, lady. I'm not in any shape to go chasing after you now."

That got her attention. Fire flashed in her eyes. "Don't you dare lay that at my feet. You got yourself into this. You're not even a real bounty hunter. Why are you involved in this at all?"

"You know why."

"Right. Taylor. You want him so bad you came down from the mountains or whatever to get him."

"Basically."

"So you're not officially on the case."

"Not officially, no."

"Funny how you didn't mention that."

"Like I said, I'm a bounty hunter and I'm after Taylor. That's all you needed to know. I don't know why you're so bent out of shape."

"I just find it interesting that you kept telling me to trust you when you weren't even telling me the whole truth."

"Life's full of irony."

"So what else haven't you told me? What other secrets are you keeping?"

"You first."

Her lips formed a mutinous line.

He pushed away from the door frame. "I'm hungry. We should eat."

"You have no authority to keep me here."

"I never did." He stared her down. "That doesn't mean I can't do it, injured shoulder or not."

He waited for her to make her move. In spite of the words, he had the distinct impression that she was in no hurry to escape. Confusion settled in again. It didn't make sense.

Or maybe it did, he thought, standing in the middle of this well-lived-in space. It would be easy to be seduced by a place like this. It felt safe. It felt like a home. Just the kind of place a woman on the run might talk herself into staying for a while.

That had to be it.

With one last glare, she turned her back to him. That look told him he'd be making dinner. He wasn't about to eat anything she got her hands on first.

BRANCATO CHECKED IN to a motel and took a long shower to soothe his battered bones while he waited for word on Ross. He'd just finished toweling off when his cell phone rang.

It was Newcomb. "No one matching Ross's description with a gunshot wound has been admitted to any of the area hospitals."

"Did you check all the ones outside the city, too?"

"Thirty-mile radius."

"So he hasn't done it yet. He will. I'll stick around here, keep checking until he does."

"What if you're wasting your time? What if he's a hundred miles away by now? We can't risk that."

"It was a good shot. It should have blown off his arm. He had to have it looked at and the bullet removed. I don't think he's stupid enough to have the woman take care of it for him." He thought for a moment. "If he doesn't check into a hospital in the next few hours, that means he knows someone here, someone he trusts enough to go to."

"I wouldn't be surprised. Ross has contacts all over the place."

"Find out who they are. I'll check every damn one of them."

"How the hell am I supposed to do that?"

"Send somebody to wherever he's been living. They have to turn up something." He stood at the window and stared out at the city. "He's here somewhere."

THEY ATE IN SILENCE. Allie devoted her attention to the photographs lining the kitchen walls, not looking at him once. Ross kept his eyes on his food. He didn't want to look at the pictures. The damn things were everywhere. Smiling faces, happy family and friends. It was enough to give a guy heartburn.

"I like your friend," she said finally, between bites of her sandwich, his culinary specialty.

He didn't respond. He shoved some food into his mouth and hoped she'd drop the subject.

"Can't see why he'd have anything to do with you, though. Looks like he's got enough friends."

Ross swallowed hard and almost choked. It would have been worth it if it'd shut her up. Damn. The woman knew how to draw blood. "He's not my friend," he muttered.

"I can see why, the way you were acting. But it's obvious he considers you one. God knows why."

He sighed. "He's my brother."

That shut her up. He might have been relieved if he thought it would stop there.

Of course it didn't. She blinked at him. "I'm sorry. I didn't think you had any family."

"Just because we had the same parents doesn't make us family," he muttered.

Her eyes widened in surprise. "That's a little harsh, don't you think?"

"It's just a fact."

"What happened? Did you have a falling-out with your parents?"

He gripped the sandwich so tightly his fingers left indentations. She was paying him back for all the questions *he'd* asked. "No."

"Just weren't close? Josh said you hadn't seen each other in a few years. I can see how you might have drifted apart, living your own lives and all that. Though if you really weren't doing anything but living on a mountain—"

He threw the sandwich onto the plate. "Look, my parents died, all right? The state split up the kids and we didn't see each other again."

He looked at the mangled food on his plate. He didn't reach for it. He'd lost his appetite.

She asked quietly, "How many of you were there?"

He wanted nothing more than to get up and walk away. Instead, he looked up and met her eyes. There was no maliciousness there. She wasn't trying to pay him back. She really wanted to know.

"Five," he said. "Five boys."

"Which one were you?"

"The oldest."

"Of course. How'd you manage to track them down?"

He raised an eyebrow at her.

She had the grace to look embarrassed. "Right. That's what you do. You find people."

He grunted and picked up his sandwich, needing something to do with his hands. "Yeah. People who don't want to be found."

"Josh seemed happy to see you."

"Josh likes everybody. As you can see."

"But not the others?"

"A couple made it clear they weren't looking to add to the family tree. I never heard from the other one."

A couple. The other one. He might as well have been discussing vague acquaintances, not his brothers.

"And that's when you retired."

"What makes you say that?"

"There was no one left for you to find."

He'd never thought about it that way. At the time it had been a combination of factors all coming together at the same time. Jed's death. The cool response from the other brothers. All he'd known was that he didn't want to do it anymore. Didn't know what else he was going to do, just that he didn't feel like chasing people down. People who didn't want to be found.

Damn her. She saw too much. It was like she could see straight through him. The way she was looking at him now.

"I'm sorry."

He shrugged his good shoulder. He didn't want her sympathy. That was the worst of all. "No reason to be. I should have expected it. We hadn't seen each other in more than twenty-five years. Everybody has their own family and lives by now. The people you were born to don't count much compared to that."

"You still have Josh."

"He's better off without me."

"How can you say that?"

He waved an arm at the photographs. "Like you said, hard to see how I fit into all of this."

He had the satisfaction of seeing her flush. "I didn't know what I was talking about."

"You met Josh. You've seen all the pictures of his smiling relatives and the people who adopted him. Do you really see me sitting down for holiday dinners with those people?" He hated the bitterness he heard in his voice, hated the sympathy he saw in her eyes.

"If they're anything like Josh, I'm sure they'd love to have you."

"No. Like I said, it's better this way, for everybody. I'm not looking to drop into some ready-made family—"

"Don't."

The anger in her voice stopped him. It blazed in her eyes, she was practically shaking with it.

"Don't sit there and expect me to understand while you pretend your brother means nothing to you. I know better. I know what it's like to lose a brother. I would give anything to have Jimmy back again. So don't pretend it doesn't matter to you. Don't pretend it doesn't mean anything. I know."

He wouldn't allow himself to feel the shame her words provoked. "You're right. It does matter. But some things can't be changed. You should also know that."

He'd managed to hurt her. He could see that. She winced as though he'd struck her and looked away, focusing her attention again on the photos.

He stood up abruptly. "I have to make a call." Reggie should have something for him by now. He needed the information, needed to get this woman out of his life.

She said nothing as he left the room.

He picked up the cordless phone from the wall and stepped into the hallway, keeping an ear on the other room. It took three tries this time to get Reggie on the line.

"What?"

He didn't react to Reg's anger. "You got what I asked for?"

The whine instantly dropped out of the kid's voice. "Oh, it's you. Boy, you weren't kidding when you said you were into something big, were you? It's all over the news here. Taylor was found dead at some rest stop in Pennsylvania."

"Yeah, I know."

"You kill him?"

"You really have to ask me that?"

"Yeah, I guess that's not your style, huh? So who did?"

"I'll let you know as soon as I do. What do you have for me?"

"What do you want first?"

"Allie Freeman," he said, more than ready to get to the bottom of what Allie was hiding.

He heard Reggie rustling papers on his desk. "She worked for Chastain's company for about three years."

Long enough for her to find out about Chastain's business practices. "Let me guess. She's missing."

"No. I have a pretty good idea where she is."

Something in Reggie's tone set off a warning bell. "Where is she?"

"Buried at St. Augustine's cemetery in Queens."

Somehow he was less surprised than he should have been. "What happened?"

"She was found floating in the East River a couple weeks

after your man Chastain was arrested for murdering the Mulroney woman. The cops tried to find a connection to the Mulroney murder, but they couldn't come up with anything."

Of course they couldn't. He'd heard that one far too often. He didn't linger on the point.

Allie Freeman was dead. Then who the hell was in Josh's kitchen a few feet away?

A vague feeling of uneasiness slid up his spine, tingling at the back of his scalp.

"Tell me about Kathleen Mulroney."

"She was in the secretarial pool at Chastain's company. Nobody important, really."

"So why'd he kill her?"

"According to computer records, she stayed late the night she was killed accessing some files in a hidden subdirectory. We don't know what was in them. Right after the murder, Chastain went back into the system and deleted or moved all those files himself, which makes him look plenty guilty. Cops still haven't managed to find them." Reggie snorted. "Amateurs. The prosecution's floating the theory that they contained proof of some of the shadier side action he had going on. Rumor has it the defense is going to counter that Mulroney was some kind of corporate spy who was selling inside information and Chastain was simply trying to undo the damage."

Ross barked out a laugh. "After he shot her?"

"From what I hear, they're leaning toward a 'temporary insanity' defense. He confronted her and lost it."

"Give me a break."

"Hey, it's a stretch, but it's not like they've got much else. The D.A.'s got him on videotape. And who's going to argue with him? It's his word against hers and she isn't talking."

"How would a secretary manage to hack into the system and dig up these files?"

"Nobody has the answer to that one. All they know is she did it. Who knows? Her brother was supposed to be pretty smart. Maybe it ran in the family."

Something in Ross went very still. "Her brother?"

"Yeah, her brother was supposed to start at Columbia in the fall, so he must have been smart, right? He worked for Chastain, too, had some kind of summer job the summer before his sister was killed."

"What happened to him?" Ross asked, even though he already knew the answer. Even though he was sure he didn't want to hear it.

"He was murdered about a month before she was. Body was found in an alley a few blocks from the subway. Wallet was gone. Police called it a mugging. Case is still unsolved."

Chapter Eleven

He knew.

As soon as Ross came back, as soon as he looked at her and she saw the expression on his face, she knew it.

He knew who she was.

He took one step into the room and stopped, simply staring at her through hooded eyes that glittered with rage.

"Allie Freeman is dead. Her body turned up two weeks after Kathleen Mulroney's murder."

He said it like he expected her to argue with him. There didn't seem to be much point in that. She slowly set down the plate she'd carried to the counter before it fell from her suddenly shaking hands. "So now you know."

"Who are you?"

"I think you already know the answer to that."

He took a step toward her. She got the sense he was holding himself back. His body shook from the effort. "I want to hear you say it. I want to know that one single thing you've told me is actually true."

"Almost everything I've told you is true."

"Everything but your name."

"I never told you my name."

She had him there. They both knew it. She could see that only made him angrier, having to grant her that one point when all he really wanted to do was rage against her deception.

The physical effort he used to maintain the tenuous hold on his temper played across his face. "Then tell me now."

Even knowing that he knew, she hesitated. She couldn't quite bring herself to say those two little words, a name she hadn't dared to speak for a year.

She took a deep breath. Her mouth formed the words that were so familiar and so alien all at once.

"Kathleen Mulroney."

His comeback was sharp and instant. "She's dead."

Everything in his tone, his expression, mocked her. Stung in spite of herself, she looked away. "So's Allie Freeman. You didn't have any trouble believing I was her."

"Because I didn't know!"

"And now you do. The only question is, what are you going to do about it?"

"What am I— Lady, there's a man on trial for killing you and you're not even dead!"

"That man did try to kill me. He shot me in cold blood and told his goons to dump my body, just like Allie Freeman's. The only reason I'm alive is because one man believed he owed me something and got me to a doctor just in time— barely—to save my life."

"Pete Crowley."

She nodded, feeling a stab of sorrow for the man who'd helped her—at great personal cost. He'd been a good man, far better than should have been working for Chastain. But then, a lot of good people had worked for Chastain, and many of them had paid for it.

"Maybe you'd better start at the beginning."

"How much do you know?"

His mouth twitched in a self-mocking smirk. "Why don't we assume I don't know anything?"

She braced herself against the counter and slowly exhaled. "You know about Jimmy. I guess that's where it all starts, anyway."

Images flooded her memory, details she hadn't let herself think about jumbled with ones she hadn't been able to forget. She struggled to organize her thoughts into words. "I told you he was set to start college in the fall. Most kids his age would have wanted to take that last summer off. He didn't. He'd had part-time jobs all through high school, but he wanted something full-time that summer. Said it was about time he pulled his own weight. So I found him something at work. It was nothing important, just your basic filing, data entry, running errands. That type of thing."

She shook her head. "I should have known he'd find it boring. After a while he started to investigate the computer system more when no one was paying attention. He was a whiz at computers. I'm sure it was nothing more than basic curiosity and wanting to see what he could do. But somehow he managed to hack into Chastain's private, highly encrypted files."

"What was in them?"

"Financial records for various illegal schemes he had going. Most of it was in a kind of code or shorthand. Jimmy had been filing building records, and he recognized some of the initials of building inspectors. It wasn't hard to figure out he was looking at a list of payoffs. Chastain was bribing them. That's what got his attention, but there was much more. Money laundering. Secret offshore accounts. Bribes to government officials. I guess when you're committing that many crimes you have to keep good records to keep them all straight.

"I'm not sure if Jimmy realized all of what he'd found, but he must have known it was big. He had to suspect they'd find out someone had opened those files, so he made a copy in case they were moved. I'm guessing it was too big to e-mail or he didn't have time to save it to disk. For whatever reason, he saved the copy on the system in a hidden encrypted file of his own so he could retrieve it later." She swallowed hard. "Then Chastain found out. The next day, he killed him."

"How can you be so sure?"

"I wasn't at first. I mean, he didn't fire me, which you'd figure he'd do if Jimmy found something and Chastain knew it. Everyone at work was really supportive and kind. But shortly after Jimmy died, my supervisor began asking me strange questions, about Jimmy, how I was taking the loss, but mostly about if he'd said anything about what he'd been working on. They acted like they were looking for some paperwork relating to an archiving project he'd been assigned to. I didn't know anything, which didn't seem to bother them for something they claimed was so important. After somebody broke into my apartment and searched the place, I got suspicious. Then I found Jimmy's notes hidden under the floorboards in his room. After that I knew what I was looking for and I went digging into the system."

"You managed to find the encrypted file?" The disbelief was back.

"Don't think a lowly secretary would be able to find her way around a computer system?" She shrugged. "You're not the only one. For all I know, that may be why Chastain didn't suspect me of knowing anything at first. I might not have gone to college, but Jimmy taught me some stuff and he left pretty good notes about where the files were. The rest I figured out on my own. Some things just come naturally."

"Why didn't you go to the police?"

"I did. I went to the detective investigating Jimmy's death and told him I what I'd found. He told me that without any proof nobody was going to believe Chastain would kill a seventeen-year-old kid. He wasn't going to take the risk. I had to get the proof myself."

"That doesn't make sense. If you brought your suspicions to the police, they should have been in the case notes."

"Maybe not. I didn't get the feeling the detective took me seriously."

"Who was it?"

"Detective Crandall?"

Ross raked a hand through his hair. "Oh, hell."

"What?"

"Newcomb, the cop who sent me after Taylor, always figured there had to be someone on Chastain's payroll inside. Hell, we all did. More than one. Crandall works out of his precinct."

It didn't surprise her. Nothing did at this point. "So instead of writing down what I told him, he called Chastain. And Chastain was waiting for me when I came out of the building that night."

"Why were you there, anyway?"

"To get the evidence of what he was up to. That night I stayed late to do the kind of search on the system I couldn't during the day, and download the files."

"Pretty risky. Even if you got away with it, he'd find out that you hadn't left the building until late."

"It didn't matter. I wasn't planning on coming back. As soon as I had what I needed, I was going back to the police. But Chastain was waiting for me when I came out the back entrance that night. He confronted me. I confronted him with what I thought I knew. That's when he told me."

His eyebrows skyrocketed. "Chastain admitted he had your brother killed?"

"No. He admitted he did it himself. You know what kind of man Chastain is. He takes betrayal personally. He killed Jimmy himself, in cold blood. That night in the alley, when he caught me, he told me everything. He bragged about the whole thing. Why not? He was feeling cocky. He'd gotten away with it. As far as he was concerned, he'd done nothing wrong. Jimmy was nothing to him, just a nobody who wasn't worthy of his consideration."

She took a step toward him, hands clenched at her sides. This time it was her voice that shook with suppressed anger.

"Do you know what he said to me? He said Jimmy wasn't worth what it cost to have his body hauled away. That's why he was dumped in an alley. Because that's where they put out the trash. And he laughed."

Even now, a year later, she could picture Chastain's face as he said it, could still hear him laughing, so damn proud of himself.

But it was Ross who stood before her. Ross whose face reflected a brief moment of sympathy before his expression hardened again.

"And when he was done gloating, he shot me.

"I only know what happened then from Pete and the newspapers. Pete and Roy Taylor were told to dispose of my body. They caught Allie Freeman fleeing the scene. I don't know why she was there, but she must have seen everything. Taylor killed her. Now they had two bodies to dispose of. They didn't want us to be found together, didn't want the deaths to be connected, so they split up. Taylor took Allie, Pete took me. From what Pete told me, I was a few feet away from winding up in the Hudson when he realized I was still alive."

"Chastain didn't bother to check?"

"The man's a neat freak. He'll pull the trigger, but he won't bloody his hands. Besides, knowing Chastain, he figured any job he did must have been done right the first time."

"And Taylor?"

"I guess I looked dead enough. Pete said he didn't bother."

"So why didn't Crowley finish you off?"

"He couldn't. He wasn't like the others. When it came

down to it, he couldn't kill a woman. Said I reminded him of his fiancée. He got me to a doctor he knew and didn't tell Chastain what had happened. He kept me hidden those first few weeks until I started getting better."

"And then? If you didn't know Crandall was corrupt, why didn't you go to the police?"

At first she could only stare at him, astonished by his blindness. Then she had to laugh. "I guess you didn't figure everything out, after all."

"What do you mean?"

"Are you really that naive? Who do you think that was out there trying to drive us off the highway?"

"You think the cops are trying to kill you? That's crazy."

"Is it? Chastain has no reason to want me dead. He needs to produce me alive in court to prove that he didn't kill me. It's the only way he's going to get off. Heck, he'll probably find a way to get out of attempted murder if I turn up. His lawyer will say I can't be trusted to tell the truth if I was willing to let an innocent man go to prison for a crime he didn't commit. The only people with a reason to want me dead are the police."

"And why is that?" Ross couldn't keep the outright disbelief from his voice.

"You said it yourself. This is the D.A.'s best chance to get Chastain on something. He's walked too many times, and they've got him dead to rights on this one. The only problem is, this is one crime he *didn't* commit, at least not successfully. Not that anyone will know that if I disappear forever."

"These men you're talking about are committed to upholding the law."

"Ri-i-ight. Because there's no such thing as dirty cops. Except this time they're worse. They're good cops gone bad out of frustration that Chastain's still walking around when everybody knows he's guilty as sin for everything under the sun. They'll do anything to get him. Who do you think killed Pete Crowley?"

"Chastain, when he found out that Crowley was going to the police. Probably thanks to somebody like Crandall."

"More like the police when Crowley told them the victim in their foolproof murder video was alive. Chastain didn't know that then. I know who came knocking when Pete was dead, and it wasn't any of Chastain's men. I know them, and I know cops. Like I said, Chastain needs me alive. It's the cops who want me dead."

"Taylor didn't seem to have any qualms about trying to take you out at the rest stop last night."

"If he was going to shoot me, my guess is he was aiming for the leg. I said alive, not uninjured. Heck, spilling my blood might have been enough to create reasonable doubt, since they have it on file from Chastain's suit and coat. Maybe they could have compared that sample to a fresh one to prove I'm still walking around. That's probably why that other man killed him. He couldn't let Taylor shoot me and have me bleed."

"What happened when these *cops* came after you?"

She ignored the twist he put on the word. "I made it out through a back window—barely. Pete had Allie Freeman's purse to dispose of. I figured she was the last person they were going to be looking for and no one knew she was dead, so the cards hadn't been canceled yet. I traded one for a fake ID with my picture and her name, and used one of the others to buy a bus ticket out of town. I've been running ever since."

"From the police."

"And Chastain's men. Detective Crandall was probably on the take. Who knows how many others there are in the police department or in the D.A.'s office? Chastain couldn't have stayed out of jail this long if he didn't have them. He eventually found out I was still alive. Maybe someone spotted me.

That's when Taylor jumped bail and came after me. With you and everybody else on his tail and mine."

She laughed. "I couldn't believe it. The one man who manages to get his hands on me out of all the people chasing me didn't even know who I was." That brief instance of humor evaporated like a puff of smoke. She met his gaze head-on. "But now you do. The only question is, what are you going to do now?"

He blew out a long, frustrated breath. "I don't know."

"Seems pretty clear. You can either let me go, or you can kill me."

His eyes flashed with denial. "Those are *not* the only two choices."

She resisted the urge to fold her arms over her chest, refusing to assume a defensive posture. She couldn't back down, couldn't let him know how afraid she suddenly was. She forced a breezy tone she wasn't remotely close to feeling. "Yes, they are. What else is there? Are you going to tell the world that reports of my death have been exaggerated?"

He was across the room in an instant, snaring her arm in a grip that immediately cut off the circulation and made her wince. He towered over her, fury radiated from his every pore. She could feel it burning into her.

"You're making jokes?" he ground out through clenched teeth. "Do you understand how much trouble you're in?"

His words only served to stoke the anger smoldering inside *her*. With a mighty jerk that nearly wrenched her shoulder from its socket, she pulled her arm out of his grip. "Of course I do. I'm the one who's been running for the past year. I'm the one who's had cops trying to kill me and Chastain's men trying to capture me for so long I can't remember when I wasn't running. You've been at this for three days. Try living this way for a year. You figure out pretty fast how much trouble you're in when you've been through what I have."

A hush fell over the room in the wake of her outburst, punctuated only by her ragged breathing. He stared down at her, amazement in his eyes, as if he'd never seen her before, as if she was a stranger. Which she was. He'd just never realized how much before now. His face was equal parts dismay and anger and disgust. He was seeing her for the first time. And she had the feeling he didn't like what he saw.

She lifted her head and met his stare. She refused to feel guilty for anything she'd done. She'd made her choices, done exactly what she had to do to stay alive and make sure Jimmy's murderer didn't go unpunished. Ross had no right to judge her. No one did. Not unless they'd faced exactly what she had.

They stood there for one interminable moment. To her surprise, he looked away first. His shoulders slumped. She'd never seen him look more tired. And just like that, the fight went out of her, too.

"Why didn't you tell me?" he asked quietly.

"I couldn't trust you. I couldn't be sure you wouldn't try to kill me."

He jerked his head up in disbelief. "Have I tried to hurt you even once in all the time we've been together, no matter how much you put me through?"

"Only because you didn't know who I really was," she said. "I couldn't trust how you'd react, what you'd do if you knew. I'm sure whoever sent you after Taylor thought they knew."

"What are you talking about?"

"Why you? Why did you get called out of retirement to chase after Taylor?"

"Because Newcomb knew how bad I wanted to see him go down."

"Exactly. They're willing to sacrifice me, they want to take down Chastain and Taylor so bad. They sent a man after you to take care of me, but they probably thought if you figured out what was really going on, you'd be more than willing to stand by and let them kill me so that Chastain doesn't get off this time."

"That's crazy. I would never—"

"Wouldn't you?" she said. "Do you remember what you said when I asked what you'd do to see Chastain convicted?"

He didn't answer. He didn't have to. They both remembered the succinct response he'd given.

Anything.

"You really thought I would kill you?"

She turned her face away. "Or worse."

"What could be worse than that?"

"You could have taken me back to New York."

He could only look at her, uncomprehending.

She could barely keep the pleading tone out of her voice. "You know why I can't go back now, don't you? If you take me back, even if they don't manage to kill me, he'll go free."

Understanding dawned on his features. "You want to see him convicted, too."

"He's a murderer."

"He didn't kill you."

"Not for lack of trying. The intent and the action were there."

"But you're still not dead."

"My brother is. Allie Freeman is. Jed is. How many people have to die before he's punished for *something?*"

She could see he didn't have an answer for that. He must have asked himself that question many times after Jed died.

She continued, "Chastain's shooting me was the best thing that could have happened. I couldn't save Jimmy and I couldn't bring his killer to justice. But I can make sure Chastain pays for what he did. And the only way I can do that is with my death. If they can't convict him for Jimmy's death, they can convict him for mine. That's the ultimate irony. And as far as I'm concerned, that's justice."

Ross gripped her shoulders. "Do you hear yourself? What are you going to do, keep running for the rest of your life? What kind of life is that?"

"What should I do, Ross? Find myself a cabin in the middle of nowhere and hide out from the world? Is that really so much better?"

She clamped her mouth shut. But there was no taking those words back. He slowly eased his fingers from her shoulders and stepped away. "You're right. I can't judge."

"I'm sorry."

"No. You made your own decisions. But if that's how you feel I don't understand why you don't just let them finish you off."

"Because I want to hear the news when he's convicted," she said. "I want to open a newspaper and see that he's finally going to pay for everything that he's done. I want to be alive when he's sentenced and taken away to prison, and I want to imagine what's happening to him in there. It's not enough that he's probably going to end up in hell. I want to *know* he's there. I want to know he's suffering, as much as he's made so many others suffer. It's not very noble. It's not admirable or forgiving or good, I know that. My mother would probably be ashamed of me, and so would Jimmy. But it's all I have left. It's all he left me with. And waiting for that day is the only thing that has gotten me out of bed every morning and kept me running. That is what's kept me alive."

She jutted out her chin and held her head high, daring him to judge her. But there were tears in her eyes, tears of anger and frustration. She didn't wipe them away, refused to acknowledge them. She saw him react to them. There was sadness in his expression, pity almost.

"And if seeing Chastain convicted comes down to letting the cops kill you so he doesn't find you?"

That made her look away. "I don't know."

He was back in her face, grabbing her arm, shaking her. "Now you *are* lying to me."

She calmly met his stare. "You're right. I don't think you'd like the answer."

His grip tightened on her arm. "You would be willing to die if it meant convicting Chastain?"

"I once said that I'd be willing to do anything to see Chastain get what he deserves, just like you. The difference is, I meant it."

"No."

She blinked up at him. Neither the word nor the fierceness of his tone made sense. "What do you mean, no?"

"I mean no. If I'm not going to kill you to see him go down, I'm damn well not going to let you martyr yourself."

"I didn't say it was the preferred option."

"It's not *any* option. We'll think of something else."

"You think I haven't tried? I've been doing this for a year. If you have any answers, I'm all ears."

"I don't. But I will."

"Why do you care? It would be easier for you to let me go and forget you know."

"In case you haven't noticed, lady, I can't let you go."

There was no sharpness in his voice, nor in the way he looked at her. The fight went out of her again. Her whole body went limp. He cupped her face in the palm of his hand and rubbed his thumb over her cheek. His hands were rough, but the touch was achingly soft. She turned her face into it, and her eyes drifted shut for the slightest of moments.

"I can't believe you thought I would kill you," he said, his voice husky.

"I didn't want to," she whispered. "You don't know how much I didn't want to."

He traced the line of her cheekbone with his thumb, his eyes reading hers. "I think I do."

She couldn't stop staring at his mouth. She remembered the way it had felt last night, had never stopped thinking about it, really. She wanted to taste him again. Fierce need pounded through her veins. She couldn't remember ever wanting anything more.

As though reading her thoughts, he lowered his mouth to hers.

This time his kiss was gentle. His lips caressed hers with the barest of touches. She closed her eyes and sagged against him as his mouth met hers in one quick, soft peck, lips meeting and retreating. Then another, quicker, more eager. Then another. Each offered a taste of something that only increased the need. Each desperate kiss led to another, each faster, longer, than the last.

He pushed her against the counter, pinning her body with the long length of his. She wrapped her arms around his neck, drawing him close. She wanted to feel him, needed to touch him.

He pulled his face away, his breathing already short and uneven. "This is probably a mistake."

The only mistake was that he'd stopped. "I've made enough of them. What's one more?"

She pushed herself up onto her toes and nipped at his lower lip. He didn't hesitate further. Their mouths mashed together in a furious assault, each taking everything they could get. Everything else, the pain, the fear, the guilt, the anger that had been her constant companions for so long, faded away. There was only this, wanting him, wanting to taste him, to feel him. It surged through her, a powerful, unstoppable force that erased all other conscious thought.

She didn't know how they made it to the guest bedroom. Maybe he carried her, his strong arms so tight around her that she didn't notice her feet were completely off the floor and he was moving them down the hall. Maybe she was so intent on relieving him of his shirt, tearing at the buttons, wanting to run her hands over the hard muscles and flat belly, that anything else was irrelevant. One moment they were in the kitchen. Then he was lowering her onto the mattress.

She sat on her knees on the bedspread. Ross pulled her fingers from his shirt and tore it off himself. Throwing it aside, he stood bare before her. She reached out and placed a shaking hand on his chest, over his heart. The hair there was unexpectedly soft. Everything beneath it was taut and hard. She caressed the muscle, savoring the feel of it, of him. She didn't even realize she'd put her other hand out until she saw it there, pale against the darkness of his body, playing against every hard ridge of his flat stomach, learning his body by touch, then moving lower…

With a soft growl, he reached for her shirt, and she froze. Sensing her response, he stopped and drew back. Suddenly she couldn't meet his eyes.

"What's wrong?" he said.

She couldn't find the words. There was no way to explain her uncertainty. She could only show him what she hadn't been able to that night in the motel.

She'd never been a vain person, never worried too much about her looks. She'd never had the luxury. This was different. This was him. So her hands fumbled as she reached down and grabbed the hem of the shirt. She took a deep breath, then pulled it over her head. She quickly unhooked her bra and dropped it onto the mattress. And waited.

She couldn't meet his eyes. She didn't want to see what she knew would be there. Pity. Disgust. Or worse, no emotion whatsoever as he covered his reaction.

He didn't say anything. Her apprehension grew with each passing second until she felt a feathery touch, so light at first she didn't realize it wasn't just the air in the room, against her chest.

With an unsteady hand, he traced the web of scars on her skin. The doctor hadn't exactly been focused on cosmetic considerations when he'd put her back together, and he hadn't had the resources of a hospital at his disposal in his small office. He may have had time to do better after she'd healed more if he hadn't been killed right after Pete. She was lucky she'd gotten what she had, she knew that. She would never be able to forget that, either, not with the permanent reminders left on her body.

His fingers moved over the scarring. They hesitated at the indentation on her left breast where she was missing a chunk of flesh that had never grown back, and lingered there.

When he didn't move, she slowly lifted her head, bracing herself for what she would see on his face. She wasn't expecting what she found.

There was no revulsion, no pity. His entire face had hardened with anger. The line of his mouth twitched from holding it in.

"I'm going to kill him for you."

All her insecurities evaporated in a flash. She almost smiled. "No, you're not." *But thank you for that.* "You're going to be too busy."

His gaze drifted upward to her face. "Oh, yeah?"

Pushing away, she leaned back on her elbows and grinned up at him. "I think so."

She watched a dark smokiness replace the fury in his eyes as he took her in. "I think you're right."

"Why don't you show me how right I am?"

He climbed onto the bed and slid over her. Leaning forward, he buried his face in the valley between her breasts.

He pressed his mouth against the scars, softly caressing them with his tongue. She gasped again, then cried out as he lapped the curve of each breast, kissing, tasting. His thumbs worked the hard points of her nipples before his tongue found them. It swirled around each peak, round and round, first one, then the other, before his mouth settled over one, hard and insistent.

She buried her hands in his hair, gripped tightly as he suckled her. Wave after wave of pleasure rocked her body. And still it wasn't enough. She wanted to make him feel as good as he did her.

"I need to touch you."

He barely moved his lips from her body. "What's stopping you?"

Her hand slid down over his stomach to cup the hard line of his arousal against his crotch. Groaning, he jerked at her touch. She massaged the solid ridge through the worn denim. He responded, pressed his body against her massaging fingers. The hardness threatened to burst through the cloth at any moment. But it wasn't enough.

She scrambled to tug his pants off. He did the same for her. Then he was in her hand, full and hard and straining. A tremor quaked through her, then through him, as she stroked the length of him. She didn't have time to savor the sensation. He growled against her throat, reaching down to rip the pants down his legs and kick them off. Then his hand was between her legs, diving into the thatch of hair he found there. A jolt of shock ripped through her. One finger probed her opening, testing her readiness. She groaned and gripped his shoulders, her fingernails digging into his skin, and heard him chuckle in response.

That one persistent finger pried apart the folds at her center, teasing her. She was so consumed by what he was doing with his mouth, with his hands, this clashing storm of feelings and sensations, that she barely registered him pushing her legs apart with his knee or moving himself between them.

She heard the distant sound of foil tearing. Moments later, he was over her, bracing himself on his uninjured arm, kissing her already swollen mouth. He was so big, it was like his body was surrounding her.

"Are you ready?" he murmured against her lips.

"Yes," she managed to say.

He thrust inside of her. He was big, she'd known that before, but he felt even bigger inside her. A sigh of rightness eased from her lungs.

He set the rhythm, and before she realized what she was doing, she was following it, meeting him stroke for stroke. She moved her hips in tandem with his, arched her back and her body against his. Sliding her hands under his armpits, she gripped him and held on as he moved them closer and closer toward a natural conclusion.

The sensation built slowly, low where their bodies met. The same pressure she'd felt before, growing in intensity until she was ready to burst. And then she did, in a liquid rush that rolled through her, one wave of pleasure after another, from head to toe. As if from a distance, she felt him tense again over her. She didn't even have the strength to hold on or tell him not to pull away. He didn't. She felt him shudder over her, rocking against her over and over again.

When they were both still again, he rolled off her. He didn't let go, but pulled her against his chest, his arm thrown over hers. They were both soaked in perspiration. It should have been uncomfortable, sticky skin and all. But it wasn't.

He pressed a kiss to her shoulder. They lay in silence for a while, the sounds of their unsteady breathing mixing in the air. She could feel his heart beating through his chest against her back. She listened to it gradually slow in time with hers.

"Still think that was a mistake?" she asked.

She felt him smile. "Maybe. But I can't say I regret it."

"Then maybe you feel like repeating it?"

His whole body rumbled under the force of his laugh, and for the first time in a year, Kathleen smiled, a true, happy smile, just before he rolled her over onto her back and kissed her again.

Chapter Twelve

Her mother's hand was soft on her cheek. The palm was rough, covered with calluses from years of scrubbing floors and cleaning with the harshest of chemicals, but the touch was gentle, barely more than a brush of fingers against her skin. Kathleen leaned into the caress, wanting more, but the hand was already falling away, as if her mother didn't have the strength to hold it up.

"I just need to close my eyes for a minute," she said. The words ended on a muffled yawn. She leaned back in the chair and looked blearily around the tiny main room of their apartment. "Did you eat something?"

"Yes." The question was familiar, the answer always the same. Her mother was always exhausted when she got home. Kathleen always tried to cook so she wouldn't have to spend more time on her feet.

She hung her mother's coat up by the door and bent down to pull her shoes off as Maura lay her head against the headrest.

"Good. That's good," she murmured. "And Jimmy?"

"He ate, too." She'd fed him as soon as she picked him up at the babysitter's.

"That's my girl."

Kathleen dropped the second shoe on the floor next to the

armchair. She looked up to find her mother watching her, her face wreathed in sadness as she gazed down at her thirteen-year-old daughter. "Such a little grown-up. I'm just going to take a nap now, okay?" she said, even though they both knew she'd probably sleep through the night in front of the TV. "You'll take care of Jimmy, won't you?"

Kathleen stood up, knowing there was only one answer she could give. "Yes."

Her mother's eyes were already drifting shut before she heard the answer. She murmured before nodding off, her voice ringing with certainty.

"I know you will. You're a good girl. You'll take care of Jimmy...."

"KATHLEEN?"

She opened her eyes and tilted her head up. Ross was peering down at her, concern in his eyes. The room was dark. It was night.

"Bad dream?"

She shook her head and buried her face in his chest. "No. Just a dream."

She felt his hands in her hair, his fingers gently massaging her scalp. She wondered if he realized he was doing it.

After a long moment, she murmured, "Tell me about your cabin. Is it nice?"

He yawned before answering. "It's not much. Just one room. But it's secluded. Nobody around for miles. Nothing but trees and quiet. It's peaceful there."

"It's in the woods?"

"In the mountains."

An image grew in her mind, so vivid she could almost believe she'd been there. Sunshine dappled the lush ever-greens that spread in every direction. Snowy peaks jutted above them in the distance. And in the center, a little square log cabin, smoke floating from the chimney into the wide blue sky. "It sounds like heaven."

"It is…"

"I wish I could see it someday."

He didn't hear her. He'd already drifted to sleep.

She was glad. She didn't want him to think he owed her anything, didn't want him to make promises she neither expected nor believed he would keep. She didn't know what tonight meant. She'd lived day-to-day too long to count on anything lasting until tomorrow.

For tonight, though, it was enough to be here, beside him. She closed her eyes and snuggled against him. His arm automatically tightened around her, almost possessively. She tried not to think much of it. He'd probably do the same with a pillow if he felt one in his sleep. It didn't mean anything.

She listened to his heart beat in his chest and savored the feel of him, and fell asleep dreaming of heaven, in the form of a cabin in the mountains where there were no people around for miles.

BRANCATO STARED at the TV without seeing it for most of the night. He couldn't sleep. He couldn't do anything while Ross and the woman were out there but wait.

His phone finally rang at six in the morning. He rose, already reaching for his coat before he took the call.

"What took you so long?"

"Ross lives in the middle of the goddamn mountains. Do you know how long it took me to find the place in the middle of the night?"

"What did you find?"

"A name. An address he had written down. Somebody he knows in Philadelphia."

"Give it to me."

Brancato scratched out the information on a piece of

paper. He hung up as soon as he had it down. Folding the paper in half, he tucked it into his coat pocket. He was heading for the door within seconds, checking his gun on the way.

It was time to finish this.

HE'D NEVER SEEN HER LIKE THIS. But then, he'd never really seen her until now.

Ross watched Kathleen sleep, so completely at peace he couldn't bring himself to wake her. Something about seeing her this way, her face calm and serene, the angry lines between her eyebrows smoothed away, a near smile curving her mouth, made his chest hurt. She was curled up at his side, her arms flung around him. She looked so goddamn trusting he didn't want to look at her. He also couldn't look away.

She stretched her limbs, making a small, satisfied sound in the back of her throat. It was the first sign she was waking up. She also managed to rub her naked body up and down the side of him while she did it, and he was hard again. Hell, he'd been half-hard from the moment he'd woken up and seen her there, her hair spread out in a cloud across his chest, completely bare. He was an old man, too damn old for her at any rate, and she had his body reacting like he was a kid again.

He was so focused on his body's response to her that he didn't notice when her eyes blinked open and met his own. "Good morning," she whispered, her voice so heavy it was clear she wasn't quite awake.

He couldn't bring himself to return her smile. It hurt too much to try. "Morning."

She slid her bare leg up and down along his, curving her knee into his. It muddled his already foggy brain. All he wanted to do was to pull her tight against him and bury his mouth on her swollen lips, forgetting about everything that faced them outside these four walls. He couldn't do it. He couldn't forget that there were people out there trying to kill her while she lay here next to him.

He hated himself for what he had to say. It couldn't be helped. He had to say it.

He nudged her softly when she would have closed her eyes again. "We have to get going."

She smiled, still half-asleep. "Where we going?"

"Back to New York."

That woke her up, as he'd known it would. Her eyes flew open. In one fluid motion, she pulled the sheet up to her chest and shoved away from him. He felt a moment's regret when her breasts disappeared from view. Her expression was wounded, her eyes gleaming with anger and more than a hint of betrayal.

"I thought you understood," she whispered, her voice shaking. "I can't go back there."

"I understand you can't keep running forever."

Her chin lifted in defiance. "I can if I have to."

"And if you don't?"

Her eyes narrowed with suspicion. "What do you mean?"

"What happened to the disk?"

"What disk?"

"You said you were at Chastain's company that night downloading the information you found. It was on a disk, right?"

"Right," she agreed. There was a distinct wariness in her answer, as if she were afraid to admit that much.

"So what happened to the disk? Did Chastain take it?"

She frowned. "Not before he shot me. He took the printouts I had, but the disk was in my back pocket. I don't even know what happened to those pants. I assumed Pete disposed of them with the rest of my clothes."

"He would have gone through them first, right? Would have found the disk?"

"He would have mentioned it."

"And if he didn't know what it was?"

She shook her head. "I think you're stretching here."

"Maybe. But if there's a chance that disk is out there and it could put Chastain away for something else and you could be off the hook, we have to follow it."

"It sounds like a long shot."

She was right. It was a long shot. If anyone had come to him with a plan this harebrained, he would have laughed at them.

Right now, he'd consider any option he had.

"It's a chance."

He didn't like the sadness in her eyes one bit. "One I can't afford to take. If I go back there on some wild-goose chase and somebody finds me, it's over." She shook her head. "I'm sorry." She pushed off the bed and rose to her feet, the sheet clutched to her body. "I'm going to take a shower."

He shifted off the mattress, following her. "If not this, then we'll figure out something else, but you have to go back to New York and face this. There has to be a way out, someone we can trust with your story so the truth comes out. We'll find it."

She cringed at his words, as if they physically pained her. "You don't know how much I wish I could believe that. I just can't take the risk."

He couldn't let it go, couldn't have explained the urgency squeezing his chest. "Is this really the life you want, Kathleen? Running until you die?"

"What's the alternative? Even if I do go back and tell the truth, I'll only live long enough to get Chastain off. At best he'll get attempted murder, and you know he'll send someone after me the second the trial's over. Then who am I supposed to turn to? The police who want me dead now? Either way, I'm running."

"You can tell them about Allie Freeman. They can convict him for her murder."

"It's hearsay. I wasn't there for any of it. I only know what Pete told me. And besides, if they have him on tape shooting me and I'm still walking around, what are the chances they're going to convict him for her murder?"

"Damn it, there has to be a way."

"There is," she said calmly. "I keep running. Chastain goes to prison for murder. I get to stay alive."

"Or be a goddamn martyr."

If he'd hoped to piss her off, he'd failed. She shrugged. "It's better than dying for nothing. Do you know why I stopped worrying about telling you details about my life after I realized you didn't know who I was? Because if you didn't, then there was no way you could put it together. I read all the newspaper stories after my 'murder.' Not one of them ran a picture. None of them mentioned anything about my life except in connection to Chastain. None of them mentioned Jimmy. No one even connected his death to mine. I couldn't even find an obituary. It was all about Chastain. This all is about him. Alive I can't do anything, but dead I can bring him down."

He started to object. She cut him off. "It's not self-pity. I'm not looking for sympathy. I'm being realistic. I'm doing what I have to do. Do I wish it wasn't the case? Of course. But it is what it is. And unless you figure something out that I haven't—something that's more than just a dangerous risk—it's how it has to be."

She went for the door. He called after her. "I don't accept that."

Her shoulders slumped. Something in the pose was so hopeless it shook him more than anything she could say. "I'm sorry," she said. "I told you before. There's nobody here to save."

JOSH'S BACKYARD was little more than a fenced-in square of grass that barely fit a barbecue and a skinny tree. It still made for a nice view. Kathleen stood at the kitchen window with a cup of coffee admiring the quiet scene, a breeze rustling the leaves, the morning sun warm on the grass.

She wished she could soak in even the slightest bit of that peace. It didn't work. The urge to flee was too strong, her uneasiness about standing here, doing nothing when she could be putting miles between her and her pursuers, too palpable.

Ross had known that, of course. He'd taken her bag into the bathroom with him when he'd gone for his own shower.

She wanted to damn him for it, even as a small part of her wasn't sure she would have been able to leave him, no matter how much she knew that was exactly what she had to do, would have to do eventually.

But not now. It seemed wrong after the night they'd shared. The memories burned through her, bringing a flush of heat to her face. God, even thinking about it, about him, brought an ache to her belly. She wanted more of him. More than that, she wanted back that closeness they'd shared. Things were back to how they'd been before last night. The tentativeness. That uncomfortable feeling of two people who didn't know how to act around each other.

She had been at peace when she'd woken, and happy. He'd had to ruin that for her, throwing around his crazy ideas. Tempting her with magic solutions she wanted to believe in more than anything, and knew she couldn't. Nothing was that easy.

Behind her, she heard the door leading to the garage open. Josh must be back from the hospital. She quickly summoned a smile to cover her emotions and turned to greet him.

The smile died on her lips. She froze.

It wasn't Josh.

A man stood in the open doorway. Triumph and hostility shone in his wide-set eyes. His sharp features gave the impression that he was sneering, though his lips were set in a thin line. She had no trouble recognizing him as the man from the motel parking lot.

Just as she had no trouble identifying the gun in his hand.

He used it to motion toward the counter. "Put the cup down."

Weighing her options, she didn't seem to have any choice but to obey. She did it slowly, watching as he glanced behind her.

"Where's Ross?"

She felt a jolt of alarm break through her shock. *Ross*. She couldn't let him hurt Ross.

"Gone." The lie slid off her tongue so easily she almost believed it.

This time there was no mistaking his sneer. "Nice try. Why don't we just wait for him to show up?"

"Why bother? It's me you want."

"Maybe at first. Now I want the both of you. That bastard's caused me enough trouble. He's got something coming to him."

His finger twitched on the trigger and she knew he was going to shoot Ross. Her heart pounded at the thought of Ross walking into an ambush. She had to distract him.

She folded her arms over her chest and stared at the man. "So who do you work for? Chastain?"

He pulled a face. "Hell, no." She was almost surprised he didn't spit after saying it. "This is all about nailing that bastard."

"Then I guess you're the good cop gone bad."

Another voice cut off whatever the stranger was about to say. "Officer Brancato isn't a cop anymore, and he was never that good."

The gunman jerked to find Ross standing in the hallway, hair still damp from his shower. Quickly shifting to keep them both in his line of sight, he centered his narrowed eyes on Ross. "You know me?"

Ross didn't move a muscle, but she sensed the coiled tension inside of him, just waiting for its moment to break free. The man must have noticed it, too. He kept his gun firmly focused on Ross.

She knew exactly what he'd done, diverted attention away from her onto himself. Her tension jumped to a fever pitch.

"I read an interesting story about you in the papers a while back," Ross said, his tone easy, conversational. "Those police brutality charges can be a pain, huh?"

"Those bastards got what was coming to them. Just like Chastain's going to."

"And Miss Mulroney? Is she getting what's coming to her?"

"After all the trouble she's caused?" He shot her a look of sheer hatred that nearly made her take a step back. "You should have died easy when you had the chance, because you sure as hell aren't now."

That split second of inattention cost him. Ross lunged for his weapon, slammed an elbow into the man's gut and took possession of the gun before he so much as glanced back in Ross's direction.

Ross stood over the man, fury radiating from every rigid inch of him.

"You're lucky the lady is standing here, or you wouldn't be alive long enough to say another word."

Clutching his stomach, the man bared his teeth. "Newcomb didn't warn me what a pain in my ass you were going to be."

A flash of uncertainty and something almost like sadness passed over Ross's face. "Newcomb sent you?" he said, an odd note in his voice.

Before she could call out a warning, Brancato had a knife in his hand, pulled from behind his back. He lunged for Ross and the weapon at the same time. The blade cut a slash across

Ross's midsection, leaving a jagged line through his shirt. She barely managed not to scream as blood appeared in the opening, straight across his chest.

Obviously expecting Ross to loosen his hold on the gun, the man grabbed for it. Ross didn't let go. The knife swung down again, right for Ross's arm. Ross caught the man's arm in his opposite hand and bent it back. The knife flipped out of Brancato's hand, landing harmlessly a few feet away.

Still they grappled for the gun. Four hands wrestled for it, tearing and clawing for possession.

A gunshot cut through the air.

She stood as frozen as the scene in front of her. Nothing moved, not her, not the men, not time itself.

Then Brancato began to laugh.

Horror swept over her. Her heart came to a dead stop in her chest.

No.

A split second later, he sagged against Ross, slowly sliding down his body until his knees hit the floor. Ross tried to bend with him to ease his fall. He released the man as soon as he rolled on his side onto the kitchen tile.

There was a hole right in the middle of the man's chest, straight through his breastplate. And blood, so much blood it seemed to gurgle from the wound as she stared in horror.

The whole time he continued to laugh, big, booming sounds that echoed off the walls and filled the small room, then slowly grew weaker, more unsteady. She didn't know what was worse, the laughter or the hacking that followed it. He began to cough blood, spitting long, dark strings of it.

He never took his eyes off Ross, who stood over him, his own face impassive.

"That bastard's still going down," he wheezed. "He's not getting off this time. They're not going to let him."

He laughed again. Blood pooled in the crevices between

his teeth, leaving his mouth a ghoulish red. He was still grinning that terrible smile when the life went out of his eyes, evaporating like the smoke from a snuffed out candle.

Silence hung in the air and neither of them moved for what seemed like an eternity.

Finally Kathleen shot forward. She kept her eyes off the man on the floor, focused entirely on the gash bleeding on Ross's midsection.

She moved to his side. He still hadn't moved. She gently put her hand on his arm. The arm that still held the gun in his right hand.

"Are you okay?"

He slowly lifted his head. The eyes that stared back at her were blank. She let her hand drop to her side.

"They're not going to stop, you know," he said. "Until they find you or until you're dead, they're just going to keep coming, one after the other. There's always going to be another just like him."

"I know."

"Is that really how you want to spend the rest of your life? Running from men like this?"

The sound that pulled itself from her throat was barely more than a whisper.

"No."

"Will you let me help you?"

It wasn't fair of him to ask her this now, not when the horror of believing he'd been shot was still strumming through her veins and rattling her bones. Not when she could smell him, the clean, spare masculine scent of him filling her head with impulses that short-circuited her thought processes. Not when all she wanted to do was throw her arms around him and have him hold her close again.

There was only one answer she could give.

"Yes."

He remained impassive, but she didn't miss the contained flicker of relief that passed across his stoic features. She slowly lowered her eyes and looked away.

She didn't add the caveat at the end. She didn't have to. It hung in the air as surely as if she'd said it aloud.

She would let him try it his way.

For now.

Chapter Thirteen

Kathleen changed the sheets on the bed in the guestroom. Ross wrapped the body in them.

Ross had pulled the car into the garage yesterday before dinner, so he didn't have to worry about anyone seeing him transferring Brancato's body to the trunk. He didn't want to leave it in the house for Josh to find. His brother was already more involved than he wanted. They also couldn't risk the police, who would raise all kinds of questions they couldn't answer. Ross checked the man's wallet, careful not to leave prints anywhere on the body. He wasn't wearing a ring. They both assumed he had no family that would miss him. Expending that much effort was more than they owed the man.

Ross mopped up the blood from the floor, washed the dishes they'd used and returned everything to where they found it. He also carefully wiped Brancato's knife and gun clean and kept them with him. When they pulled out of the garage, they left a house that was spotless and silent.

Ross waited until they were deep into New Jersey before pulling off the highway. They traveled down a series of increasingly deserted access roads until they found one he must have deemed desolate enough. She started to get out of the car. He waved her back in, hefted the body out of the trunk, and disappeared into the trees with it. He returned a few minutes later, alone. She didn't ask what he'd done with the body. He didn't tell her. He didn't have to.

Neither of them said a word the rest of the way into New York. There didn't seem to be anything to say.

KATHLEEN FELT NO SENSE of homecoming, no wave of nostalgia, as they passed over the bridge into Brooklyn, where Reggie Harris was waiting to meet them. Ross had called him before they left Philadelphia, telling him what they needed to know. He'd promised to have it by the time they arrived.

She watched the streets pass by with a strange sense of detachment. This wasn't the area where she'd grown up, but the buildings, the people they passed, were still familiar. This was home, or at least close enough.

And she felt nothing. It felt no more like home than any of the cities she'd lived in briefly over the last year. The only thing that distinguished it from the others was the uneasiness growing in the pit of her stomach the farther they drove into the borough. It was a prickly sensation dancing along her nerve endings, her instincts shouting out a warning.

She shouldn't be here. She should be far, far away, as far as she could get. This was a mistake.

But one she was willing to take, for reasons she wasn't sure she wanted to examine.

Reggie Harris lived in a third-floor walk-up in a modest apartment building located not far from Prospect Park. Ross parked five blocks away, and they wound their way through a series of alleys to the rear of Reggie's building. They'd stopped just long enough on the drive into the city for hats and sunglasses, anything to serve as some semblance of a disguise. Ross still checked inside before motioning for her to follow. It was the middle of the day. There was no one in sight. She still felt exposed in the open air.

Ross placed a calming hand at the small of her back. "You

okay?" he murmured, low enough that only she would be able to hear him.

"I'm fine," she lied. "Let's get this over with."

Reggie took his sweet time answering the door. Muffled curses echoed through the door as he slid all the locks and chains free. The pale face, complete with a shock of dyed white hair and bloodshot eyes, that glared out at them through the crack in the door verged on skeletal.

His gaze shifted from Ross to her and back again. The ferocious expression eased somewhat, though not by much. He swung the door open halfway and waved them in. "I don't know how I'm supposed to get anything done with you bothering me every five minutes."

The rest of him was just as thin and white as his face. He was all scrawny, jittery limbs that never stopped moving. She could see why he had so much trouble with the multitude of locks. His hands were shaking badly.

She shot Ross a look.

He shook his head. "He's fine. Just a little intense."

Reggie finally finished with the locks. Ross quickly introduced them. "Kath, this is Reggie Harris. Reggie, this is Kathleen."

The man's head bobbed up and down a half dozen times. "The dead girl? Cool."

Before she could be taken aback, he dodged around them and led them down a cramped hallway that was closed in further by the floor-to-ceiling shelves that lined it on both sides. Every inch of shelving was packed with computer equipment and miscellanea, all glowing ominously in the dim pathway.

The living area, if it could be called that, he led them to wasn't much better. Heavy curtains blocked out the sunlight from the windows. Instead the room was lit by the unnatural glow of several computer monitors on the desk and the halogen lamps perched over them. The artificial glare was blinding after the shadowed darkness of the hallway. Music blared from a set of old-fashioned headphones left abandoned on the desktop.

Reggie threw himself into the desk chair. Unsurprisingly it seemed to bear the permanent imprint of his rear end.

"Did you get the information I asked for?" Ross said.

He whipped around in the chair, paper in hand. "Crowley's fiancée's address, as requested."

"You got a picture?"

"What kind of slouch do you take me for?" Reggie groused, sliding a computer printout of a driver's license photo into Ross's hand.

"Great. Is it okay if Kathleen stays here with you while I go talk to this woman?"

Reggie's eyes went so wide she was surprised they didn't slide out of the sockets. Apparently he found the idea about as comfortable as she did. Kathleen wasn't surprised. She'd bet good money she was the first woman to set foot in the apartment since he moved in.

"Her? Here? Why?"

"We can't take the chance someone will see her on the street. This place is barricaded better than a bank vault."

She and Reggie exchanged unhappy looks.

"Don't you have anybody else? One of your friends with guns or something?"

"Nobody I trust."

Reggie grimaced. "You're a lot more trouble than you're worth, Ross. You planning on paying me for all this?"

"You ever known me to try and rip you off?"

She could see Reggie fighting back his misgivings. "Fine," he grumbled, spinning back around to his computers. "Just as long as she stays out of my way."

Kathleen shook her head. "Gee, how can I turn down such a gracious offer?"

"Don't push it, lady."

Waving him off, Ross pulled her back into the hallway. "Don't worry about Reggie. He's harmless."

"Believe me, him I can handle. That's not what I'm worried about."

"You should be safe here. I'll be back as soon as I can. Hopefully with good news."

"Hopefully," she echoed, unable to meet his eyes.

He hooked his finger under her chin and tipped her head up to look at him. "We're going to find a way out of this."

She forced herself to nod. She wished to God she felt anywhere near as confident as he sounded.

She rubbed a hand along the goose bumps prickling her arm. She shouldn't just be standing here. She should be moving.

He stared at her for a long moment, then pulled her in his arms and kissed her. She held on to it for as long as she could, wrapping her arms around him and letting it all soak in. The way he felt. The way he tasted. The way he smelled. She stored away every detail to hold on to forever, and refused to admit to herself the reason why.

He pulled away, and she already felt utterly alone.

"I'll be back soon," he said.

She nodded once and watched him go, trying to ignore the furious buzzing in the back of her brain and the almost painful knot of tension in her stomach.

A mistake. This is a mistake.

BRANCATO HAD FAILED.

Newcomb sat at his desk stewing, his tension rising with every tick of the clock. He had no proof that was the case, nothing but an instinct that told him it was true. Brancato hadn't checked in. He wasn't answering his phone. If he'd gotten the woman, he would have reported back by now. Something had gone wrong. Again.

Luckily, Newcomb had several backup plans in his pocket from the start. Ross was supposed to have been one of them. Newcomb was still fuming about that miscalculation. He'd thought Ross wanted Chastain and Taylor so bad he'd realize what had to be done if he ever found out about the woman. Newcomb still wanted to believe that Ross just didn't know, but that pipe dream was running out of steam. He had to know by now, and he didn't have the balls to do what had to be done.

Of course Taylor was dead, so maybe Ross had already gotten what he wanted done the most.

When the phone rang, he lunged for it, ignoring the glances it earned him around the squad room from a bunch of cops who'd never seen him move so fast. "Newcomb."

"Detective Newcomb? This is Adele Abramowitz. You spoke with me about one of my tenants?"

He had no trouble placing the older female voice lowered conspiratorially. Someone had been watching too many bad cop shows, in this case the manager of Reggie Harris's apartment building. She was just one person connected to Ross he'd tapped throughout the city. Newcomb knew the man was a key source of information for Ross, something Ross wasn't aware he knew.

A surge of excitement rushed through his veins. "Of course, Mrs. Abramowitz. What can I do for you?"

"You said to let you know if anyone visited Reginald Harris?" She said the name with a great deal of distaste. "I've been watching, just like you asked."

Of course she had. The nosy old bat was a shut-in. What else was she going to do with her time but monitor the comings and goings in the building?

He caught Crandall watching him from his desk. Newcomb lowered his voice and leaned into the phone. "Is someone there now?"

"Yes, a man and a woman. They sneaked in the back, like they didn't want anyone to see them. No one's supposed to use that door but residents. I think the man picked the lock."

Newcomb's blood pressure skyrocketed. Damn it. Ross had brought the woman back to New York. "Could you get a good look at the woman?" Could anyone?

"No. She's wearing big sunglasses and a scarf over her head, like some kind of movie star."

Newcomb felt a twinge of relief at that. Thank God for small favors. "All right. Keep watching in case they leave. I'll be right there."

Crandall was still watching him from his desk when Newcomb hung up the phone. "What's going on, Ken?"

Newcomb pushed himself up from his chair and reached for his chair. "I've gotta head out for a while. I don't know if I'll make it back today."

"You need me to come with?"

Newcomb shook his head. "Nah. It's kind of personal. Just something I have to take care of myself."

The way he should have all along.

MARTIN CRANDALL WAITED until Newcomb had left the squad room before rising from his chair and moving toward the exit. He didn't go in the direction Newcomb had, toward the garage. He didn't have to. He'd heard all he needed to.

Abramowitz. Manager of an apartment building in Brooklyn Newcomb had spoken to a few days ago. Crandall had been monitoring his calls, had the whole exchange on tape. The slight bit of this conversation he'd managed to overhear, Newcomb's reaction, told him all he needed to know.

Ross and the woman were in the city.

CHASTAIN WAS AT HOME when the call came. That was nothing new. It felt like he was always at home. He couldn't do business the way he wanted to do it. People were avoiding him, canceling meetings, refusing to take them. He was having to depend on his underlings. God, how he hated that. He'd had to stop going into the office, tried getting things done from home. It wasn't the same. The penthouse was starting to feel like more of a prison than the one they were threatening him with.

At least he had a few loyal employees left.

"She's here."

With those two words, Chastain's mood changed in an instant. A jolt of energy had him shooting forward in his chair. "Where?"

"Ross took her to one of his old sources in Brooklyn. They're there now. Newcomb's on his way there. You want me to go after him?"

"No. She's mine." The dead girl was too slippery. He wasn't trusting anyone else with her this time. He would get her himself.

"Give me the address." He quickly jotted it down, then hung up the phone and rose from the desk.

Kathleen Mulroney had caused him trouble for too long. She wouldn't die today; unfortunately, he didn't have a choice in the matter.

But that didn't mean he couldn't hurt her.

"WOULD YOU KNOCK IT OFF?" Reggie griped. He shot her a dirty look over his shoulder.

"Sorry," Kathleen muttered. She couldn't stop pacing. She wasn't used to sitting around and doing nothing, and the in-activity was driving her crazy.

She wasn't expecting Ross to come back with good news. All she wanted was for him to come back, so she could take every last second she had left with him.

"Don't be sorry. Just quit it."

She stopped and threw her hands up. "If you had an ounce of breathing room left in this place, I'd be happy to go there and get out of your way. But there's nowhere for me to even sit."

"The bathroom."

"Tell me you're not talking about the toilet."

"It has a lid on it."

"I'm guessing you don't have many guests over."

"Don't want 'em. They tend to be really annoying."

She'd unconsciously started pacing again, wandering the confined space of the room. She saw the flash of irritation. He opened his mouth to offer another cutting remark.

Then they both heard it.

The sound of a key sliding home in the front door.

She'd locked the door after Ross left.

They froze. Their gazes met and locked.

"You expecting company?" she whispered.

He waggled his head from side to side. "No."

"Who has the keys?"

"Only the landlady, Mrs. Abramowitz." The fear faded back into his usual scowl. He leapt to his feet. "The old bag is always threatening to come in here and check on me if she doesn't see me for a while. Figures it'll be bad for the property value if I kick it in here. I've got a million bucks in hardware in here. I don't need her poking around."

"When's the last time you saw her?"

He fluttered a hand. "A couple of weeks ago. Maybe a month. There's no reason to. Everybody delivers these days. Hold on, I'll get rid of her."

She grabbed for his arm, unable to shake the feeling that this wasn't right. "Reggie—"

But he was already gone, stomping down the hallway to the door.

"Reggie, don't—"

She couldn't see the front door from this room. She started to edge toward the only escape route, the windows. The next thing she heard was the chain being slid off the door and Reggie griping, "Listen, you old bag—" as the door opened.

Silence.

Then the sound of something heavy crashing to the floor. She held her breath, listening to it echo around her.

Then she heard footsteps, slow and careful, moving down the hall toward her.

It wasn't Reggie. There was no way that heavy, even stride matched Reggie's jittery, stuttery cadence, no reason for him to be so stealthy.

She ran for the window, even more careful to make no sound than he was being. She had no idea if there was a fire escape on this side of the building, or if the window would even open, but she had to try.

In the hallway, the man began to move faster. She tore at the curtains, only to find the shades had been taped down against the glass beneath them.

She spun around, reaching for the closest object to break through the glass.

A man stepped through the doorway. She froze.

Definitely not Reggie. He was overweight and balding, dressed in an ill-fitting suit that made him look uncomfortable. His face was heavily lined and sagged with bags and excess skin. He would have made a pathetic sight if it wasn't for the two strikingly blue eyes that burned with intensity almost directly in the middle of his head. In his hand he held a gun. He didn't point it at her. He didn't have to.

Neither of them moved. For a long while they just stared at each other. There was nothing to say. He knew who she was. She knew why he was there. He had cop written all over him.

She spoke first. "Where's Reggie?"

"He's taking a nap. He'll wake up soon. His head'll hurt but he'll be fine."

It seemed a strange reassurance to offer her, but no stranger than what he said next.

"You'll come with me, won't you?"

It wasn't really a question. They both already knew the answer.

Ross, I'm sorry.

"Yes," she said.

Chapter Fourteen

Ross couldn't shake the uneasy feeling clawing up his spine that dogged him all the way back to Reggie's. He'd blown it. He'd known it was a long shot, but he'd have given anything to come back with good news. He didn't have any. After waiting an eternity for Pete Crowley's fiancée to return home, it had taken her about two seconds to inform him that she had all his personal effects and a disk hadn't been among them. The man hadn't even had a computer, so she would have noticed a disk.

He'd put Kathleen in danger for nothing.

No, not for nothing. There had to be another way. He just had to figure out who could be trusted, who they could turn to. There had to be someone. He wasn't about to give up now.

It gnawed at him as he climbed the steps to Reggie's apartment, discouragement but not defeat.

Then he reached the third floor landing and stopped. His mind went blank.

Reggie's door, the one with the multitude of locks that should have been sealed, stood ajar.

He broke into a run, slamming through the door and into the apartment. The door met resistance with a loud thud.

"Damn it, Ross. You trying to kill me, too?"

Ross pulled the door back. Reggie was on the floor, rubbing his head.

Ross fell to his knees. "What happened? Where's Kathleen?"

Reggie winced. Only then did Ross realize he was shouting.

"Gone, I think."

"What the hell do you mean, gone?"

"We heard somebody unlocking the door. I thought it was the landlady. She's the only one who has the keys. I was going to give her hell, but it wasn't her. It was this guy. He hit me." The last words came out in a whine.

"What'd he look like?"

"Big. Older. Fat."

"Newcomb." Ross said it like a curse. "He probably flashed his badge at your landlady and got her to fork over the key."

"A cop did this? Damn. I'm filing brutality charges."

"This was outside the line of duty." Ross moved down the hall to the living room, Reggie trailing behind. He surveyed the room. "There's no blood, no signs of a struggle. She went willingly."

"Hell, if she wanted to go with him I would've let her. He didn't have to hit me."

"She didn't want to go with him. She just would have given him a much tougher time of it if it had been one of Chastain's men."

"So why didn't she give the cop any trouble if she didn't want to go with him?"

"In her mind, it's better to be caught by the cops than Chastain."

"What's he want with her?"

"To kill her."

"That's better than Chastain?"

Disbelief rang in Reggie's voice. Ross had a hard time disagreeing with him.

"She thinks so. Maybe she thinks she can escape." *For the love of God, Kathleen, try to escape.*

Reggie rubbed his scalp, wincing when he hit a tender spot. "So what do we do?"

"Where would Newcomb take her? He needs to make sure she disappears forever and no trace of her ever shows up again."

"Somewhere he can dispose of a body where no one's going to find it?"

Ross didn't let himself think about Kathleen as the body they were so calmly discussing. "Some kind of private property he knows well where no one else would go." The answer came in a flash of insight. "Jersey. He owns land in Jersey. My guess is not too far from the city. I need to know where. Now."

"That could take a while—"

He grabbed a fistful of Reggie's shirt, dragging him up off his feet. Reggie's eyes bulged. "We don't have a while. You owe me, Reg. I need to know where that property is."

Reggie held his hands up. "Okay, okay, I'll find the place."

Ross released him. "Do you have a cell phone?"

"Yeah. Why?"

"Give it to me."

Reggie looked only too happy to inch away from him. He moved over to the desk and shoved some papers around until he produced a cell phone. Ross took it and bolted for the door.

"Call me with the address."

Reggie called after him. "Where are you going?"

"Jersey."

"But you don't know where you're going."

"I'll be a hell of a lot closer when you call me than I'd be here. Get on it. Now."

He slammed out of the apartment, already running again. Damn, he didn't know how much of a head start Newcomb had. He could already be at his destination.

Kathleen could already be dead.

No. He wasn't going to let himself consider the possibility. She was a fighter. She had to still be alive.

He couldn't even manage to convince himself. He clung to the thought all the same.

"TWENTY-FIVE YEARS on the force, watching scum everybody knew was guilty walk time after time. None of them was as bad as Chastain, and we couldn't do a damned thing."

Kathleen didn't respond. Newcomb had been talking like that from the moment he'd gotten her in his car and started to drive out of the city. His right hand sat in his lap, still holding the gun. She hadn't said a word. It hadn't stopped him from continuing.

Worst of all, she was in handcuffs again.

As expected, he went on. "And he's not going to stop, you know. It's only going to get worse. Someone's got to stop him."

Kathleen watched the expressway zip by outside her window. She tried to calculate how much damage it would do if she threw herself out of the moving vehicle. Most likely she'd fulfill Newcomb's goal for him. All that would be left would be for him to go back and pick up the corpse.

There had to be some other way to escape. Maybe when they got to wherever he was taking her. She still had time.

She'd thought she'd be ready for this moment if it came to it. She'd thought she'd be ready to face the prospect of dying when it was this close. But she'd be damned if she was going to give in without a fight.

She realized Newcomb wasn't saying anything. She looked up to find him watching her in the rearview mirror, that simmering fever in his eyes. If Newcomb's behavior hadn't done enough to prove to Kathleen that his nut was cracked, the feral gleam in his eye would have done it. After the first few minutes she'd done her best to avoid looking into them. That wildness in his eyes told her more than ever that he was capable of anything.

"You understand why it has to be done, don't you?"

"I'm not sure what it is you want me to say. Do you want my permission?"

He broke the eye contact, turning back to the road. "No, I guess not."

"Can you really do it, Detective? Can you really kill me?"

"You think I haven't killed before? Don't kid yourself."

"Like Pete Crowley?"

He met the challenge in her stare without blinking. "Like Pete Crowley."

"He must have known that you were one of the cops who wasn't on Chastain's payroll and just how bad you wanted him. Did he come to you? Did you shoot him in cold blood?"

"He got what he deserved. Who knows how many murders he was in on."

"He saved my life."

His eyes narrowed to slits. "Don't remind me."

She could tell she wasn't going to win with that argument. "What about me, Detective? Is this what I deserve?"

He didn't say anything, didn't look at her. She knew she'd scored a point.

She pushed the issue. "You haven't killed an innocent person, have you, Detective? I don't believe you've done that." She took his silence for the confirmation it was. "Is that who you are, Detective?"

"You answered your own question. I'm a homicide detective. My job is to find slime like Chastain and get them off the streets."

"Within the law."

He slammed his fist against the steering wheel. "I tried. We all did. This is all I have left, and by God, I'm going to do it."

"Because Ross couldn't? Is that what you thought he'd do, Detective? Kill me when he found out the truth?"

"I didn't want him to know if he didn't have to, but yeah. I figured it'd be good to get someone who hated Chastain as much as the rest of us, someone who'd know what it would take to get the bastard."

"You underestimated him."

"I overestimated him. I didn't think he'd lose his head over a piece of tail. So now I have to take care of things."

She couldn't even work up the indignation to be offended. She couldn't ignore how eerily familiar the words were. "Even if it means becoming no better than Chastain?"

"One death compared to dozens. I still have quite a ways to catch up with Chastain."

"Murder's murder, Detective."

"Except Chastain does it for himself. I'm trying to save people. Think of how much safer the world will be with that bastard behind bars."

Kathleen closed her eyes against his words. The scariest part was knowing that just days ago she probably would have agreed with him. Nothing mattered more than seeing that Chastain finally got what was coming to him. She would have been ready to make that sacrifice.

But not anymore. Now she knew that not even vengeance was worth this. But most of all, she didn't want to die. For the first time she could remember, her own life meant something to her.

"You don't have to do this. There's a disk out there with the files I copied the night I was shot. The financial records prove Chastain's illegal activities. There's enough to put him away."

His laugh mocked her. "Right. Even if I believed there was some miracle evidence out there, it's not good enough. All the deaths that son of a bitch has caused and he'll get a couple of years in a country club prison for what? Some white-collar crimes? Give me a break. This is the way it has to be. This is the only way."

Considering how she'd felt less than twenty-four hours ago she could hardly argue the point.

There had to be a way out. She had to find it.

"I'm right," he muttered. "You know I'm right."

The miles raced by, taking them farther and farther from the city, from Ross. She wondered who he was trying to convince, her or himself.

ROSS CHECKED EVERY VEHICLE he passed as the car ate up the miles into New Jersey. It was too much to hope he'd catch up to Newcomb, but he still clung to the possibility. It was better than the alternative, thinking that he might be headed in the wrong direction altogether.

Or that Kathleen was already dead.

No, that wasn't even a possibility. It couldn't be.

His cell phone rang. He grabbed it before it could ring a second time. "Tell me you have it."

"I have it." Reggie rattled off the address. "You need directions?"

"Give them to me just in case."

Bracing the phone between his shoulder and chin, he scratched out the directions on a piece of paper on the seat. He wasn't sure they'd be legible. At least he'd have them.

"Thanks, Reg. Call the New Jersey state police. Tell them there's a hostage situation, a woman's life is in danger, and send them there."

"Got it. You're sure he's taking her there?"

"I'm not sure of anything. But it's all I've got."

He hung up the phone and tossed it aside, slamming down on the accelerator until it hit the floor. He was still a good thirty minutes from Newcomb's property.

He intended to make it in ten.

THEIR FINAL DESTINATION was an undeveloped tract of land somewhere off the highway in Northern Jersey. Bordered by drooping trees on all sides, it was a quiet spot. Traffic from the highway was barely more than a faint hum in the distance. Under other circumstances, she might have found it peaceful. Appropriate enough for a place that was intended to serve as her grave.

Newcomb parked by the trees and cut off the engine. "Get out." He pulled the key from the ignition and started to climb out on his side.

She hesitated, gauging the likelihood she could slam his door shut and lock it before he could stop her. Then, if she could hot-wire the engine—

He stopped half-in and half-out of the vehicle and glared at her. "I said get out."

He motioned toward the door with his gun hand for extra emphasis. She had no choice but to obey.

He never took his eyes off her as he moved around to the back of the car and unlocked the trunk. He picked up a shovel in his free hand, then slammed the trunk shut with his elbow. For some reason the shovel was more intimidating than the gun. The weapon was a possible threat. The tool was far more concrete evidence of how real the threat was.

Newcomb waved toward the trees with his gun hand. "Now go."

"Where?"

"Over into the meadow."

She did as ordered, though her eyes never stopped moving. Could she risk darting into the trees? She might make it a few feet, but he'd be right on her tail. It was still a chance. She could just run, as fast as she could. Would he shoot her in the back? Was he that kind of man? Could she take the chance? Could she chance not doing it?

She felt him come up right behind her, pushing the barrel

of the gun into her spine. She jerked forward. He never moved the gun, jabbing it harder into her back.

"Move."

Then they were in the meadow. The cold weather had already killed the grass and it wasn't high. The late afternoon sunlight shone down over the area in a warm orange glow.

A nervous laugh bubbled in her throat. She couldn't have chosen a nicer place to die.

They only went a few yards into the meadow. She felt the gun disappear from her back.

"Turn around."

She did. He stood a few feet away, the gun still aimed at her, the shovel clenched in his other hand. He let it drop. Neither of them paid any attention to its fall.

He didn't say anything. His jaw was still clenched with grim purpose, but in the dying light she saw for the first time how tired he looked. He looked like all the energy had been sapped out of him. And she knew she had a chance.

There was no reason for him to delay, no reason not to get it over with.

He made no move to do so.

"You don't have to do this," she said, trying to sound as calm as she could with a gun pointed at her, his finger lying heavy on the trigger.

"Yes, I do."

"I want to see Chastain pay for everything he's done just as much as you do. We'll find a way."

Anger sparked in his eyes. "There is no other way. Five years I've been chasing him down, catching bodies with his name all over them. You think I wouldn't have figured something out if there was something besides this?" He shook his head heavily. "Why couldn't you just stay away? Why'd you have to let them find you?"

"I can hide again."

"And let them catch you again? No. This ends now."

He said it with such finality she couldn't help but take a step back. "You don't want to do this. It's not who you are."

"You know who I am? I'm just a cop who's tired of Chastain and his garbage. It's time to end it."

He clicked off the safety and aimed the gun straight at her head.

She couldn't move. Couldn't speak. Couldn't do anything but stare down the barrel of the gun.

She expected the shot. She expected the explosion that rocked the trees and echoed through the meadow, deafening her. Still, her whole body went rigid from the shock of it.

She didn't expect Newcomb's eyes to go wide or his mouth to fall open in surprise. It worked silently, forming words that never came.

He pitched forward and fell in a heap at her feet.

Blood oozed from the back of his coat. She could only stare at it for an endless moment. She forced herself to lift her eyes.

Price Chastain stood a few yards away, the gun in his hand now aimed at her. He paid no attention to the man he'd just killed, the body in front of him on the ground.

He looked only at her, his face rigid with suppressed anger.

He smiled.

"Hello, Kathleen."

Chapter Fifteen

He didn't look any different. They could have been standing in that alley again more than a year ago. He had the same patrician handsomeness unmarred by stress or age lines, the same coolly arrogant expression. It was as infuriating as it was disappointing. She'd expected—hoped, really—that he would show some evidence that the last year had been as hard on him as it had been on her. He should at least look somewhat worse for wear. It was only right. It was only fair.

That was what she got for clinging to one last hope that something in all of this could possibly be fair.

His voice was the same, too. She remembered it well. It dripped with condescension, the king lowering himself to speak to a commoner and not about to let her forget it.

"Well, well. Kathleen, alive and well, at last. You know, you've been quite the pain in my ass the last few months."

She said nothing. She couldn't force the words out, couldn't do anything but stare at this man who'd destroyed her life. She'd thought she hated him before. Only now, standing there, the bitterness of it burning through her like hot acid eating away at her insides, did she understand just how much she hated this man.

He stepped out into the open, a small smile playing on his

lips. "That's odd. You don't seem happy to see me. I must say I'm very happy to see you."

"I'm sure you are," she ground out.

She grew more rigid with every step he took that brought him closer. "You must have heard about this pesky trial I have coming up. For some reason the authorities seem to believe I murdered you."

"I wonder where they got that idea."

He continued as if she hadn't spoken. "It's funny. You must have heard, and yet you did nothing to help me out of this mess."

"Did you really think I would?"

He feigned astonishment. "Why, yes. Your brother seemed to believe rather strongly in doing the right thing. I thought he must have gotten that from you."

It was all she could do not to launch herself at him and knock that coy smile off his face. "Don't talk to me about my brother."

"What was his name again? Jimmy?"

"Don't you *dare* say his name."

The first hint of rage cracked through his conversational air. He shed the pretense. The smile faded, twisted into a sneer. "That was always your problem, Kathleen. You never knew your place. You or that worthless brat. Here's a reminder. I'm the one with the gun. I can say whatever the hell I want and you will listen."

"The hell I will." She took no small satisfaction from the way his eyes widened briefly in surprise. Sending him a confident smirk of her own, she began to move toward the trees, one step at a time.

He never let her out of the weapon's sights. "Get over here."

"No."

He cocked the gun and aimed the barrel at her head. "I said, get over here."

"Or what? You'll shoot me?"

"Do you really want to tempt me, Kathleen?"

"I know you won't kill me. You need me alive. It's the only way you can prove you didn't kill me that night."

"Doesn't make any difference to me whether you show up alive or freshly dead. Either way everyone will know you didn't die a year ago."

"Right. You drag a corpse into court, everyone is going to know you did it this time."

"I don't need to produce you in court to prove the point. All I need is to ensure your body pops up in a very public place. You forget. I'm very good at having bodies dumped so they cannot be connected back to me."

"But not so good at making sure they're really dead."

The way his expression twisted, she was surprised when she didn't find herself with another bullet in the chest.

Instead he kept following her with the gun. "It may be more advantageous for you to still be alive. That doesn't mean I can't put bullets in a few judicious places. Who would blame me? After everything you put me through? A little temporary insanity would easily be justified. I may even be able to convince the hapless idiots in the police department that it wasn't me who shot you. Your word against mine, and you aren't exactly trustworthy, are you, Kathleen? After all, you've lied to everyone all this time about being dead."

She should have known something was up the way he kept talking, should have seen in the sudden shifting of his eyes to the side. Warning bells went off in her head, causing her to slow her movements. She didn't understand why at first.

Then his smile was back.

"Or else I can shoot him."

She watched in horror as he whirled in a forty-five degree angle, aiming his weapon at a new target, the man who'd just stealthily moved out from the trees behind him into the clearing.

Ross.

She froze. She couldn't have moved if she tried.

He had a gun in his hand but it wasn't lifted. He'd never be able to get off a shot first.

She hadn't been afraid before. Chastain could shoot her, but he couldn't kill her. That gave her power. That gave her a chance.

Now she knew what fear was.

Her gaze locked with Ross's. In his eyes she saw all the terror she felt for him reflecting toward her in return. She wanted to scream at him across the distance, wanted to rail at him for putting himself in danger for no reason.

Except she knew the reason. She would do the same for him. And that was the most terrifying thing of all.

"Drop it, Ross," Chastain ordered, swinging the gun back on her. Her relief was short-lived. "I might not kill her but I can damn well take off a leg."

She shot Ross a look. *Don't do it.*

I have to, came back loud and clear. He let the weapon tumble from his fingers.

The sound of the gun landing on the ground was cut off by Chastain's laughter. "How about it, Kathleen?" he crowed. He backed up to keep them both in front of him, shifting his attention between them. "Let's see how good you really are. You can come willingly, or you can run while I kill Ross here. If anyone deserves a bullet between the eyes more than you, it's him. What'll it be? Are you willing to let someone else die to save your own skin?"

"Don't do it, Kathleen," Ross called, his voice calm and sure. He exhibited no fear in his demeanor. Only in his eyes did she see it. Fear for her.

There really wasn't even a choice.

"I have to," she said, unable to keep her voice from shaking. "He's going to kill you."

"Kath—"

"Ross, do shut up," Chastain smirked. "Let the lady make up her own mind."

"I have." She couldn't bring herself to look at Ross anymore. She forced herself to focus on Chastain instead. "I'll come with you if you let him go."

She knew immediately she'd revealed too much. His eyes narrowed on her face, his gaze coolly assessing. A malicious gleam entered them, one she'd seen before.

She knew what he was going to say before he said it.

"Idiot. You're coming with me either way. Like you said, I need you."

And he smiled.

"But I have no reason to keep him alive."

Time slowed to a series of beats, each second a snapshot of a moment that lasted for an eternity.

Ross inched forward, not yet having processed what was about to happen.

Chastain's smile deepened.

She opened her mouth to scream.

His jaw set, Chastain jerked toward Ross.

Ross froze.

It couldn't have been more than a few seconds. She saw every moment with the clarity of slow motion.

This was it.

This was everything.

She was watching Chastain kill Jimmy, a defenseless boy with nowhere to hide and no place to go.

She was back in that alley on a rainy night, at the end of the barrel of that gun herself, knowing she was going to die, knowing there was nothing she could do to stop it.

She was here, watching a man she knew without reason that she loved about to be killed.

Except this time there was a gun inches away.

Before the thought fully formed, she was already moving, lunging for Newcomb's weapon. Heart exploding, the roar in her ears deafening, she jerked to her knees and thrust the barrel in Chastain's direction.

And pulled the trigger.

The explosion shook her to the bone. For a split second, she thought her arms had been pulled from their sockets. She somehow stayed on her knees.

Chastain's body flew backward in a wide arc that lifted him off his feet. Blood sprayed from his upper body. The arm with the gun was flung upward, away from Ross, toward her.

She saw Chastain's gaze settle back on her. His face was contorted with rage, the amusement wiped clean. He began to lower his weapon in her direction, aiming at her.

She braced both hands on the gun and pulled the trigger.

His body spasmed, jerked back and forth under the force of the explosion. A cloud of crimson exploded from his shirt. He screamed, a horrible high-pitched squeal that echoed in the clearing. Pain twisted his features into a mask of agony.

Their eyes met across the distance. Hatred burned in his.

He didn't know what hatred was.

And she pulled the trigger.

ROSS SAW CHASTAIN'S WEAPON moving in his direction a split second too late.

He braced for the impact.

It never came.

Gunfire echoed in his head, one shot after another. Every muscle in his body tensed, expecting the explosion of pain, the sharp sting of bullets impacting flesh, tearing at muscle and bone.

The noise in his ears began to recede. He finally noticed the only pain he was feeling came from every inch of his body being clenched in readiness.

The fact penetrated. He was alive, unhurt.

His vision cleared, just in time to see Chastain standing unsteadily on his feet, the front of his shirt drenched in blood, his face a mask of shock, the blankness in his eyes indicating he was already dead, before his body finally toppled backward into a heap on the ground.

Stunned, Ross immediately sought out Kathleen. She was on her knees right where she'd been before, a gun in her hands. Her finger continued to reflexively work the trigger, again and again and again, though the chamber was long out of bullets.

Forcing his limbs to move, he went to her and gently placed his hand over hers.

"He's dead."

It took a few moments for the words to register. Her finger slowed on the trigger, and her grip eased enough for him to slide the gun from her hands. Her eyes never wavered from where Chastain lay. Her stare was unblinking.

"Good."

The word was flat and emotionless. As soon as it emerged from her mouth, she began to shake all over. Tremors racked her body so hard he immediately dropped the gun and fell to his knees and grabbed her before her legs could collapse out from under her. He knew the signs. She was going into shock, and it was no wonder. She'd no doubt dreamed of killing Chastain a million times in the last year. The satisfying fantasy did nothing to prepare a person from the actual act of taking another life.

She clung to him, and Ross held her close. He didn't say a word. He simply held her, until the sirens began to echo in the distance and the police finally started to arrive.

Chapter Sixteen

The graves lay side-by-side near the edge of the cemetery. Neither had any kind of headstone or marking. It didn't matter. That would be taken care of soon enough.

Kathleen was still thankful that she'd managed to make the burial arrangements for Jimmy before that long-ago night and everything that had followed it. Losing him to a bullet had been hard enough. Losing him to a potter's grave would have only made it harder.

Evening fell in rapidly stretching shadows across the lush greens of the cemetery. There was no one else around. She was glad for that. She welcomed the time alone with her mother and Jimmy. She could almost feel them there with her.

That was only part of the reason she lingered at the graves long after darkness crept over them, hiding them from view. The other was knowing Ross was waiting for her back at his truck, waiting for the conversation they'd both been avoiding.

The time had come to say goodbye.

When it finally grew so dark she could barely see the ground in front of her, she leaned forward and pressed a hand to the soil, whispering a promise to return. It was one she would keep.

If only anything else was as certain.

Ross was waiting for her at the bottom of the rolling hill.

His profile was a reassuring sight. She felt that lurch in her chest she always did when she saw him. She savored the moment one last time.

"You okay?"

He must have mistaken the emotion he read in her face. She did her best to hide it. "I'm fine. The headstones will be installed next week."

"Nice of the mayor to give you that settlement without even having to ask."

Her smile was grim. "He just wants me to go away, and the story with me." For weeks the papers had been dominated by news of rogue and dirty cops in addition to the demise of the much unloved Chastain.

His lips curved upward the slightest bit. "I figured that had something to do with it."

"I am glad, though." The money also had allowed her to pay off the charges she'd made on Allie Freeman's credit cards. The D.A., who also very much wanted the story to go away, had agreed not to prosecute her for fraud, one more relief. "It'll be nice not having this drag out further. I can start to move on, figure out what to do next."

He shoved his hands in his pockets. "Yeah, you can. Any ideas on that front?"

They stood there in uncomfortable silence for a few seconds, as night closed in around them.

She shrugged. "I don't know. Everything's been so crazy lately…"

"I'm sure you want to get back to normal now."

"There's nothing for me to get back to. My old life is gone. My job. My family. I can do anything I want to."

"And what do you want to do?"

This was it. "That depends. What are you doing?"

For a moment, she saw something shift in his features, something hopeful, quickly covered.

He sighed and shook his head. "I don't have anything to offer you."

"I think you do."

"I don't know what the hell I'm going to do with myself for the rest of my life."

"Neither do I."

"I don't much like being around people."

"Who needs them?"

"I'm too old for you."

She smiled. "Forty's not much older than thirty-three."

The joke seemed to take the fire out of his arguments. He moved closer, until she could see his eyes, glowing faintly in the moonlight. "All I know is I didn't go to all the trouble of saving your life to watch you walk out of mine."

"I seem to recall being the one with the gun in my hand while you were on the receiving end of one."

A faint, rueful grin touched his lips. "Then it sounds like I'd better keep you around, just in case."

"Sounds like a good idea to me."

She held her breath, almost afraid to believe.

Finally, after one long, heart-stopping moment, his expression eased. He smiled.

Then she was smiling, too. And for the first time in so long, she felt something she hadn't thought she ever would again, an emotion so foreign it took her a moment to realize what this particular feeling was bubbling forth inside.

Hope.

The smile still on his lips, he stepped back and held out his hand. It was more than an offer. It was a promise.

She didn't hesitate. She slipped her hand into his, and together they disappeared, once more, into the night.

* * * * *

The editors at Harlequin Blaze have never been afraid to push the limits—tempting readers with the forbidden, whetting their appetites with a wide variety of story lines. But now we're breaking the final barrier—the time barrier.

In July, watch for BOUND TO PLEASE by fan favorite Hope Tarr, Harlequin Blaze's first ever historical romance—a story that's truly Blaze-worthy in every sense.

Here's a sneak peek...

BRIANNA stretched out beside Ewan, languid as a cat, and promptly fell asleep. Midday sunshine streamed into the chamber, bathing her lovely, long-limbed body in golden light, the sea-scented breeze wafting inside to dry the damp red-gold tendrils curling about her flushed face. Propping himself up on one elbow, Ewan slid his gaze over her. She looked beautiful and whole, satisfied and sated, and altogether happier than he had so far seen her. A slight smile curved her beautiful lips as though she must be in the midst of a lovely dream. She'd molded her lush, lovely body to his and laid her head in the curve of his shoulder and settled in to sleep beside him. For the longest while he lay there turned toward her, content to watch her sleep, at near-perfect peace.

Not wholly perfect, for she had yet to answer his marriage proposal. Still, she wanted to make a baby with him, and

Ewan no longer viewed her plan as the travesty he once had. He wanted children—sons to carry on after him, though a bonny little daughter with flame-colored hair would be nice, too. But he also wanted more than to simply plant his seed and be on his way. He wanted to lie beside Brianna night upon night as she increased, rub soothing unguents into the swell of her belly, knead the ache from her back and make slow, gentle love to her. He wanted to hold his newly born child in his arms and look down into Brianna's tired but radiant face and blot the perspiration from her brow and be a husband to her in every way.

He gave her a gentle nudge. "Brie?"

"Hmmm?"

She rolled onto her side and he captured her against his chest. One arm wrapped about her waist, he bent to her ear and asked, "Do you think we might have just made a baby?"

Her eyes remained closed, but he felt her tense against him. "I don't know. We'll have to wait and see."

He stroked his hand over the flat plane of her belly. "You're so small and tight it's hard to imagine you increasing."

"All women increase no matter how large or small they start out. I may not grow big as a croft, but I'll be big enough, though I have hopes I may not waddle like a duck, at least not too badly."

The reference to his fair-day teasing was not lost on him. He grinned. "Brianna MacLeod grown so large she must sit still for once in her life. I'll need the proof of my own eyes to believe it."

Despite their banter, he felt his spirits dip. Assuming they were so blessed, he wouldn't have the chance to see her thus. By then he would be long gone, restored to his clan according to the sad bargain they'd struck. He opened his mouth to ask her to marry him again and then clamped it closed, not wanting to spoil the moment, but the unspoken words weighed like a millstone on his heart.

The damnable bargain they'd struck was proving to be a devil's pact indeed.

* * * * *

Will these two star-crossed lovers find their sexily-ever-after?
Find out in BOUND TO PLEASE by Hope Tarr, available in July wherever Harlequin® Blaze™ books are sold.

HARLEQUIN *Blaze*

Harlequin Blaze marks new territory with its first historical novel!

For years readers have trusted the Harlequin Blaze series to entertain them with a variety of stories— Now Blaze is breaking down the final barrier— the time barrier!

Welcome to Blaze Historicals—all the sexiness you love in a Blaze novel, all the adventure of a historical romance. It's the best of both worlds!

Don't miss the first book in this exciting new miniseries:

BOUND TO PLEASE
by Hope Tarr

New laird Brianna MacLeod knows she can't protect her land or her people without a man by her side. So what else can she do—she kidnaps one! Only, she doesn't expect to find herself the one enslaved....

Available in July wherever Harlequin books are sold.

Silhouette® Desire

HIGH-SOCIETY SECRET PREGNANCY

Park Avenue Scandals

Self-made millionaire Max Rolland had given up on love until he meets socialite fundraiser Julia Prentice. After their encounter Julia finds herself pregnant, but a mysterious blackmailer threatens to use this surprise pregnancy and ruin his reputation. Max must decide whether to turn his back on the woman carrying his child or risk everything, including his heart....

Don't miss the next installment of the Park Avenue Scandals series— *Front Page Engagement* **by Laura Wright— coming in August 2008 from Silhouette Desire!**

Always Powerful, Passionate and Provocative.